GIDEON

Boyfriend For Hire, Book 3

RJ SCOTT
MEREDITH RUSSELL

Love Lane Books

Gideon, Boyfriend for Hire, Book 3

Copyright © 2021 by RJ Scott

Copyright © 2021 by Meredith Russell

Cover design by Meredith Russell

Edited by Sue Laybourn

ISBN: 9781785645419

RJ ~ Always for my family.

Meredith ~ For my family and friends for their continued love and support. And thank you to RJ for allowing me to create another beautiful story with her.

Boyfriend for Hire
GIDEON

RJ SCOTT & MEREDITH RUSSELL

Love Lane Books

ONE

Gideon

"I, Darcy Jonathan Bridges…"

Gideon glanced at the select group of guests in the intimate venue in New Canaan. Darcy and Adrian exchanged their vows in the small room full of white flowers and with an arch decorated with greenery. The wedding was a simple indoor service with no more than twenty people, all of whom had been handpicked to attend by either bridegroom, consisting of their immediate family and the closest of friends.

So why am I here?

Gideon was Darcy's boss, but he still wasn't sure how he'd ended up being invited to the wedding. He was convinced that his PA, the annoying but sexy Rowan Phillips, had simply decided they were both attending and barreled ahead with the plans. Rowan had organized hotel rooms for them both only a short taxi ride from here, and insisted that staying over was all for Darcy and making the day special. More likely Rowan wanted to drink copious amounts of alcohol, but there again maybe he had the right idea. Gideon glanced toward where Adrian and Darcy were standing hand in hand. A drink or three to get through the day was probably in order so a hotel was for the best.

Ceremony, dinner, celebrations, alcohol, staying overnight, then in the morning it was off to *somewhere* for the newlyweds and back to the office on Stuyvesant Street in Manhattan for Gideon and Rowan. Gideon had work to do, contracts to assign for next year's events and last minute checks on Christmas events given it was only nine days away.

There would be the inevitable last minute panics for work parties or family events, and he recalled a request for a two week booking covering a huge family's New Year gathering at a location in Vermont. While lucrative, the Vermont booking had been left way too late because backstories for the people he hired were complicated matters for long-term connections, and he never put his employees in situations they couldn't handle.

He'd have to turn it down, but that wasn't an issue. Bryant & Waites was solid, financially secure, and discreet, all the things he and Luke had planned the company would be.

And there it was. He'd thought about Luke and he knew he should stop focusing on the past. Just because he was at a wedding, and twenty years ago Luke and he were supposed to go to Canada and get married and be together forever…

Think about Rowan instead.

No, don't think about Rowan. Not sexy, in my face, snarky, coffee making Rowan.

Christmas. *Yeah, I'll think about Christmas. The commercial stuff. I can do that.*

Rowan shifted next to him, their hands brushing, and all kinds of forbidden thoughts rushed to his head. He and Rowan holding hands, he and Rowan kissing, he and Rowan…

Christmas decorations, music on repeat, parades, more gift cards to buy. He began to make a mental list of what he could handle in the run up to the usual meeting with family for the big day. He wanted the decks cleared so he wouldn't be dragged under by family stress. His oddly matched and long-time divorced parents bickering about who'd get him and his sister for which part of Christmas. He was forty-three for fuck's sake, his sister only a few years younger, and yet the two of them were still fought over as if they were small kids. Not to mention Gideon's birthday fell on Christmas Eve, which made things even worse. Typically, he hid away on his birthday if he could manage it, but last year he'd spent it with his sister and her boyfriend, and that in itself had been a different kind of chaos.

"They look so happy," Rowan said as he leaned into Gideon briefly.

"Uh-huh," was about all Gideon could manage. He'd been lost in thought and anyway, no one should be talking at weddings.

"I might get married here," Rowan added, and Gideon shot him a surprised glance.

"You're getting married?" he asked louder than a whisper and got an irritated stare from another guest.

Rowan raised an eyebrow. "Of course."

Shock flooded Gideon as they turned back to face the happy couple. He hadn't even known that Rowan was with someone, let alone at the point where they were thinking of getting married. What if Rowan left Bryant & Waites? What if he left Gideon to run the company on his own? That didn't bear thinking about.

What if Rowan leaves me?

Rowan moved again, this time a full body sigh as Darcy and Adrian exchanged a vow. He smelled wonderful, a fresh citrus scented cologne that reminded Gideon of the ocean.

"Who's the lucky guy?" Gideon murmured as everyone began to clap and whistle at something.

"Huh?" Rowan said as the clapping died away.

"The man you're marrying."

Rowan tapped his nose then winked. "Now that would be telling."

Great. Just when things were level and the company was steady, Rowan was running off with the first fly-by-night asshole who gave him a ring. Gideon could already picture some smooth city banker or a lawyer who had bought Rowan's affections with gifts and empty promises —just to take him away from Bryant & Waites.

And me.

The thought of gifts reminded him that he still hadn't bought Rowan a Christmas gift, which was a slap to the face. There was this rich city guy, probably showering Rowan with gifts, winning his heart, and

Gideon hadn't even considered the measly Christmas gift he usually bought his PA. It was the only one that he bought himself because the gifts to the other guys who worked for him were handled by Rowan himself. Not that Gideon would have to think about what to get him. Because Rowan would likely happen to leave an open magazine on his desk with some very specific comment on a Post-it.

At least Gideon knew that Rowan was getting something he wanted.

I bet Big-city guy doesn't know Rowan as well as I do.

The countdown to Rowan leaving him had clearly begun, but he couldn't stop the march of time. What was the point in dismissing the fiancé he'd never met when he himself had never actually made a move on his PA? Well, not a real move.

Focus. He needed to focus on the here and now, glancing briefly at Rowan, right by his side as usual. His suit was a deep blue color, standing out next to Gideon's gray. His tie a bright orange, Gideon's a silver-blue.

Rowan had once told him that blue ties made his eyes pop, whatever that really meant, but Gideon certainly hadn't worn it so he popped his eyes at anyone today. Particularly not cheerful perky Rowan who smiled so wide his nose wrinkled and who was clearly getting married. Gideon had to ignore that Rowan looked good today, bright and smiling, and so different to how he was dressed in the office. His dark hair was newly cut, carefully layered, and his brown eyes were wide with an almost childlike wonder. He had a sprig of holly in his buttonhole, a nod to the season that was reflected in some of the decorations in the room, and he looked... attractive?

That was possibly the safest description that an employer should use about their newly engaged assistant because sexy, gorgeous, fuckable, and hot were not the words he should be using. Along with cute, always sunny, but sometimes disrespectful and irritating. Rowan was stuck in Gideon's head, and the time had always been coming when they would need to part ways before Gideon's idiot-attraction went from bad to worse. Maybe in the new year Gideon could ask Rowan to find a replacement for when he left with his husband...after paying Rowan handsomely for his time of course.

Since the first Wednesday in October at ten thirty-two in the morning, his and Rowan's working relationship in the same office had started to become very different.

Rowan had hugged him. In Rowan's defense, it had been the day after Gideon had taken his cat Kimi to the veterinarian. The hug happened out of sheer relief when the news came in that a lump the vet had found was just an infection. Although he wasn't sure if it had been Rowan or himself who instigated it.

The feel of Rowan in his arms was a memory he would never lose.

Stupid libido and its ability to fuck with my head.

"Maybe I'll get married on Christmas," Rowan said softly as the vows or whatever drew to a close. He had his fist on his chest, right over his heart, and were those tears in his eyes? Rowan loved all things Christmas.

The only buffer between Gideon and warring

divorced parents at Christmas was his sister, Grace, and what a flimsy buffer she was. They weren't close at the best of times, but she was dating this guy who had the weirdest nasally tone to his voice and wouldn't stop talking about how much of Gideon's wealth he would love to invest. Maybe the problem was he reminded Gideon too much of their own father. No matter the situation with his family, everything came back to money in the end.

So while Gideon dreaded the season and its family obligations, Rowan counted down the days with an advent calendar filled with chocolates and chatted endlessly about this brother or that sister or what his moms had planned. This was the same PA who Gideon could guarantee would already have a Christmas playlist on his phone. He'd dance to the music as he filed or made coffee or even as he walked out for lunch. As of yet Rowan hadn't put in his earbuds to play it when there were no clients in the office.

Not that Gideon checked.

Okay, so I checked.

There was an unspoken rule for respectful silence in the rarefied air of the offices of Bryant & Waites. At least, it had been an unspoken rule until what had become The Lady Gaga incident, and now it may as well be in huge letters in every contract. Returning unexpectedly to the office after a late meeting, Gideon had found Rowan with his earbuds in, singing along to the music he was listening to and dancing like an idiot in the kitchen. After he'd stood and watched for a good few minutes wondering what to say, Rowan had turned and spotted him. He'd explained there was no one in the building but him, adding something about the floor being polished, and that he wasn't wearing shoes because he could slide better.

Gideon listened to it all and then, ashamed that he'd been caught watching, blew everything out of proportion and gave some lecture about solemnity and silence being the watchwords of Bryant & Waites. His face heated as he recalled that night because Rowan took the comments to heart and was as quiet as a mouse for at least two weeks until it became so quiet that Gideon was slowly driven mad. He'd left a Post-it note on Rowan's desk apologizing for overreacting, and they'd never spoken of it again.

Although he still couldn't get the image of Rowan dancing, or the hug, out of his mind.

Rowan was life and happiness and being in everyone's business while totally efficient, and he fixed everything so Gideon had an easy life. He was the perfect PA and a thorn in Gideon's side all at the same time.

He needed to stop thinking about Rowan getting married and leaving him, or recalling the way he moved, and his off-key singing, and how sexy he'd looked when—

Cats. Think about my cat. That's safe.

I hope Kimi's not too pissed that I'm away tonight.

Not that Gideon's beautiful Ragdoll cat would be angry at his absence, she loved Hilda, his neighbor, and was probably being spoiled right now with fresh salmon and unending treats.

"Earth to Gideon," Rowan whispered, and Gideon blinked down at him, seeing the twinkle in his brown eyes. "I can see the thought bubble from here," Rowan added as the small group of people began to clap and Gideon joined in, although why he was clapping he didn't know, then belatedly realizing that somehow he'd missed a vital part of the ceremony. Darcy and Adrian were kissing and then hugging, both grinning at each other as if they were the happiest people on earth.

Did I even hear Darcy and Adrian say their I Do's?

"Don't start with that bubble shit," Gideon warned. Rowan had this *thing* where he would draw an oval shape in the air with extended fingers and then state what he thought Gideon was contemplating. Unfortunately, nine times out of ten he was right.

Rowan smiled. "You were thinking about something completely unrelated to the ceremony, and then you pondered about important clients, and finally you ended up thinking about your cat."

Gideon ignored Rowan and stared back at the happy couple, after all the laughter in his PA's eyes was way too alluring, far too beautiful of a thing, and he wasn't going *there*.

"I was making a mental list of agencies who supply replacement personal assistants," he said instead, trying for humor and realizing it worked when Rowan snorted with laughter, the noise lost in the clapping that continued on for a long time as Adrian and Darcy kissed and hugged their way around their friends and family.

"You'd have to find a magic agency." Rowan leaned in and got far too close, and Gideon knew he should have kept his mouth shut, but no...he fell right into Rowan's trap.

"What do you mean a magic agency?"

Darcy had nearly reached them, but there was enough time for Rowan to shrug and bite back a laugh.

"Only PAs capable of magic can handle the ogre in the main office."

"You're fired—"

"And rehired, obvs." Instead of the word obviously, he'd started using "obvs" recently. It was *obvs* to everything as if correcting Gideon when he messed up by using the annoying shorthand made things better.

"Guys, thank you for coming." Darcy was there, shaking hands, bro-hugs, a much longer hug for Rowan, but then again, the two men had been friends for thirty years. Adrian caught up with Darcy, dragging him into a kiss.

"Hey, husband," he said.

"Hey back, husband," Darcy said, and they kissed, right in front of Rowan and Gideon. So close that Gideon could see the tender way Adrian cupped Darcy's face and the emotion that had them leaning on each other, with the absolute certainty that neither would let the other fall.

I want that. I really want it.

He was trapped in his quiet corner, hemmed in by the kissing, laughing newlyweds and Rowan, who was grinning so hard it had to hurt.

When the two separated, they all hugged again, and this time it was thank yous for the gifts. Gideon hadn't known what to get them. Adrian wasn't wanting for money, and what did you buy two guys who had their own place? He'd settled on a generous gift card to an upmarket bespoke furniture showroom, and they seemed pleased, explaining they were sure they would find something perfect there, and for a brief moment, Gideon felt as if he'd done something right in a social setting, and that he was a good guy.

But Adrian was gushing all over Rowan. "How in the hell did you know about the rare Ella Fitzgerald pressing?"

Rowan winked. "I have my sources," he said and brushed at his shoulders indicating that he was a freaking genius.

"You mean Darcy told you," Gideon said and laughed because he'd made a joke, but Rowan shook his head and looked serious.

"I never said a thing," Darcy said.

"No, he didn't. You remember that barbecue we had at yours? You said that she was one of your heroes, and you loved her music, and then we were talking about it after, and you mentioned you were looking for a particular version—"

"Oh God, I did, how the hell do you recall that?" Adrian hugged Rowan. Again. There was way too much hugging going on, and Gideon remained trapped in the corner.

"You know I'm a genius," Rowan deadpanned, and Gideon bit back the need to make a barbed comment about how his PA had probably written it down in his journal, but that wasn't really a joke and would have made everything awkward.

"And the dogs," Darcy said. "Thank you." He hugged Rowan, and Gideon was less worried about *that* hug. Them being friends and all.

"What dogs?" Gideon asked because firstly, he was trapped, and secondly, he'd promised himself to make a real effort at this wedding.

He never did get an answer because someone yelled from the other side of the room about toasts and food and a party, and it was as if the tide that had been washing toward Gideon suddenly reversed, and it was only him and Rowan left.

"What dogs?" he repeated.

"Darcy and dogs have been a thing for a while I guess. You probably don't know but he used to volunteer at a dog sanctuary, donated to a Dogs for Veterans charity. I think he's still in touch with some ex-army buddies who had worked with the K9 unit. So, yeah, I donated in his name." He made it sound as if it was nothing, but his gifts were thoughtful, personal, whereas Gideon didn't even know the two men well enough to come up with anything cleverer than a generic gift card.

"Come on." Rowan tugged Gideon to the door through which everyone had left. "I don't want to miss out on champagne!" The smaller room decorated with simple flowers opened up into a bigger room with a few round tables, a large cake, and horrifically, a dance floor. Gideon nearly turned and ran. He could face down multinational corporations, defend his staff and friends to the death, discuss terms with the richest families in the US, and sometimes in foreign countries. He could maneuver his way through the trickiest of negotiations and shield his company, but the thought of a dance floor, which meant dancing?

Nope. Not happening.

Gideon deliberately chose a table near the door—for a swift exit—then changed his mind when that was also too close to the dance area then went to the back but quickly realized he'd be hemmed in again, and then he simply just stopped walking.

"Here, boss." Rowan encouraged him to sit, and in Rowan's capable way, he'd found a seat equidistant between dancing, cake, and freedom. He didn't ask Gideon why he was standing there like an idiot. He just dealt with it, but they weren't at work. This was a social situation, and Gideon wasn't a freaking idiot.

"I can find my own damn table," Gideon snapped.

Rowan blinked at him and pointed at the table in front of which they were standing and a small card that had *Gideon Bryant* handwritten on it. He was sandwiched between Adrian's sister, Abby, and Rowan. Sitting in his chair, he settled in for whatever happened next. Well shit, he hadn't seen the card.

"Sorry," he murmured.

Rowan smiled at him, in reassurance maybe?

"S'okay boss. Here, have some champagne."

Maybe I shouldn't drink? Maybe I should stick to water and then I could keep my head and not ask Rowan why the hell he's marrying some guy I've never even met.

But the champagne sure tasted nice.

TWO

Rowan
_____

*I'm not bothered. It doesn't bother me...*Rowan ran his index finger around the rim of his champagne flute as he fixed his gaze straight ahead. He nibbled his lower lip. Gideon was fidgeting with his phone.

I'm lying. It definitely does bother me. The phone had rung a few times and each time Gideon picked up the phone, huffed, and then canceled the call before turning the phone upside down as if he didn't care.

"If you're not going to answer it, just turn it off." Rowan picked up his glass and took a long drink.

"I can't *just* turn it off," Gideon said with a sigh and placed his cell phone face down on the low coffee table. Again.

The grooms were off on an intimate photoshoot, and the guests were left to their own devices as music played in the main room.

"Who are you avoiding anyway? It's you, so it's definitely nobody work related. Oh, do you have a stalker? Maybe a secret lover?" Rowan knew he sounded a little too excited about those possibilities but *Nosy* might as well have been his middle name.

Gideon shook his head and made a gruff sound. "Who the hell would want to stalk me?"

Rowan leaned his head. "Well, if I had nothing better to do." He laughed.

"How are last month's accounts coming along?" Gideon looked at him pointedly.

With a chuckle, Rowan finished his drink and got to his feet. "Would you like another drink?"

"That well, huh?" Gideon quirked an eyebrow at Rowan's obvious attempt to swerve the topic of work.

With a smile, Rowan leaned down and looked into Gideon's blue eyes. "Have I ever let you down?" He cast his eyes downward, briefly lingering on Gideon's lips, noting the stray gray whiskers in his neatly trimmed beard, before settling on the pale blue tie tucked beneath his buttoned waistcoat.

"Maybe you should slow down with the alcohol," Gideon suggested, sitting back.

"Or maybe you should speed up," Rowan teased. He pursed his lips. He felt odd. Something fluttered in his chest. Maybe Gideon was right.

Too many bubbles with lunch.

"I'm fine, really," Rowan said and straightened up. "I'm just loosening up for the dance floor." He glanced at Gideon, who stiffened as if Rowan had just made a threat on his life. "It should be a good night, right?" He knew full well that the idea of dancing the evening away was far from anything Gideon would consider a "good" night. "Oh, maybe they'll take requests. I could totally go for some Gaga right about now."

Gideon cleared his throat and looked anywhere except at Rowan.

Definitely too many bubbles. Gaga had been off limits all this time and all Rowan could think was w*hy did he even say that?* He didn't want things to be weird between them again.

"Or maybe Beyoncé," Rowan added quickly to drive his one-sided ramblings forward. "But it is almost Christmas, so Mariah would be perfect." He picked up his empty glass. "Anyway." *I really need to shut up.* "Are you sure I can't get you anything?"

Gideon reached for his glass. "Maybe later." He raised his drink to his mouth and for a moment Rowan was mesmerized by Gideon's parted lips.

Alcohol is the devil. His brain was focusing on all the wrong things. Wrong, bad, terrible things.

Maybe Mom and Momo are right, and I should find myself a man. He walked to the bar, glancing back at Gideon. Yeah, he needed to find a man—any man who wasn't his boss.

Returning to the table and setting his drink on it, they fell into an easy silence, or at least it should have been easy apart from Gideon staring at him every so often.

"What? Do I have something on my face?" Rowan asked after the fourth staring session.

"Who is he? Is he a client? You know you shouldn't marry clients." Gideon frowned as he spoke.

"Wait—are you saying you have an issue with Darcy

and Adrian marrying? Because you know technically Adrian wasn't a client—"

"No, of course not. It's *you* I have an issue with."

"Huh?" Rowan was bewildered at Gideon's statement.

"I have an issue with you crossing a line and marrying a client."

"Okay. Then I won't."

Gideon sighed noisily. "Well, who is he then and how did you meet him?"

"Who's who? I'm confused."

"The man you're marrying on Christmas."

"What man?"

"You said you were getting married, and you wanted it to be on Christmas."

"Gids, I was talking hypothetically."

"It's Gideon, and good." Gideon huffed and deliberately turned his chair to face away from Rowan, pretending to stare out the window.

Interesting.

"I need a drink and then dancing," Rowan said and that ended the subject of Gideon getting the wrong end of the stick.

At some point in the evening Rowan found himself dancing with Darcy's mom. He hadn't seen Katy Bridges in almost twenty years. Not since he and Darcy graduated high school and ventured out into the big world and onto separate life and career paths.

Though, somehow, we ended up together again in the end.

Being around Katy felt weirdly nostalgic. Rowan remembered his old house, how he and Darcy had become friends in kindergarten, not long after he was fostered by Mom and Momo and then adopted.

Twenty years, huh?

Had it really been that long? His foster parents moved the year before he left home, wanting more space inside and out for the children they took in. Christmas time at their house was a large jumble of people, and he found himself going back every year, he and the kids who had been adopted and had become his siblings. That feeling was everything to him. Family. Seeing Katy and talking about times back then elicited that same warmth, and it was as if he was a teenager again, the same swell of excitement rising in his chest as the times he and Darcy would sneak out to meet at night, doing the things teenagers found themselves doing.

I was a bad influence.

Rowan made his way off the dance floor, stopping at the bar before walking back to the table. He took a long drink of soda. Hiccupping as the tepid fizzy liquid hit the back of his throat. He noted the empty chairs, and for a moment wondered if Gideon had given him the slip and headed to the hotel. No. His jacket was still hanging on the back of the chair.

Where is he? Rowan checked his cell phone. Should he call him? Or would that be weird? He wasn't Gideon's PA tonight, and Gideon was a grown-ass man who could do as he pleased.

But we're friends. And this friend was curious where the other had run off to.

Rowan pocketed his cell and eyed Gideon's jacket. Doubt crept in.

Are we friends? Or was work all they had? Did it matter?

Alcohol caused ridiculous questions to spiral around his skull.

Whatever Gideon was to him, all Rowan knew was that he kind of cared about him, and the fact Gideon had been avoiding calls all evening had him annoyed, curious, and a little bit concerned.

I should look for him.

He didn't have to search for long. Rounding a corner, Rowan found Gideon leaning against a doorway overlooking a small patio. Gideon had his back turned and was on his cell. His free hand cradled his chest against the December air that blew in through the open door. Rowan kept his distance, backing away and dropping into a chair against the wall to wait.

"You're really ditching me this year?" Gideon said. "Yes, I know you two just got back together, again. I—"

Rowan leaned his head against the wall and listened.

"Sis, I get you want to be with him, but his family as well? You hate them, even he hates them. Sorry, hate is maybe too strong a word but—what?" Gideon gave a hollow laugh. "Money. Of course, that's the reason. So, it's another get rich quick scheme, and he thinks he can talk his brother into investing? Yeah, I thought so."

Rowan shifted in his seat. He shouldn't be listening to this. Gideon never really talked about his family. It had been the same for Kaden. Seemed family was complicated for both of them.

"I've told you before. If you need money, I'll help you. *You*. But I won't support any of his flights of fancy.

No, I'm not trying to start a fight. There's plenty of that with Mom and Dad. I know. No. Just forget what I said. I'm sure you'll have a great time. Yes. It's fine, I'll figure something out. Just…you know where I am if you need me." His tone was laced with defeat. "Bye, Grace."

What should I do? If he stayed there, Gideon might catch him and that would be damn awkward. Rowan mustered the courage to lean out of his seat and checked around the corner just as Gideon stepped outside. The translucent drape bellowed in the open door and Rowan could make out Gideon's silhouette beneath an exterior light on the patio.

Sitting here won't solve anything. He stood, fastened the button of his vest, and followed after Gideon.

"Oh, there you are," he said as if he'd found Gideon by chance. "I thought you'd ditched me for that cute waiter from dinner." He kept his tone playful.

"Cute waiter?" Gideon asked as he brought up his shoulders.

Rowan shook his head. "Never mind." He breathed in sharply through his teeth and rubbed his shoulder. "What are you doing out here? You'll catch your death." He stepped closer, bumped his elbow to Gideon's. "Then who would keep me in line?"

With a chuckle, Gideon glanced up at the sky. "I needed a minute."

"Is everything okay?"

There was a pause, but Gideon eventually said, "Yes. I'm fine. It was just getting a little stuffy in that room." He took a deep breath and turned to face Rowan properly. Despite his smile, there was an air of something that left Rowan on edge.

"Did you want something?" Gideon asked as they headed back inside. "You seemed to be having fun when I left."

"Nothing really. You weren't at the table, so I thought I'd take a break and look for you."

"Well, you found me."

The music grew louder as they made their way along the corridor.

Rowan tugged the back of Gideon's shirt, bringing him to a stop. He knew if they went back in that room the music would drown out the ease of their conversation. But Rowan couldn't think of a single thing he wanted to say, other than wanting to be near Gideon to make sure things really were all right with him.

I want him to know I care. And yet, I don't.

"Do you want a drink?" he suggested.

Gideon shook his head. "I think I've had enough."

Rejected.

Heat rose in his cheeks. "Right. Erm…bathroom." Rowan waved his hand in the vague direction of the bathrooms. "I'll see you later?"

"You okay on your own?" Gideon raised his eyebrow as Rowan pressed his hand to the wall to steady himself.

Rowan laughed. "I think I can manage."

"I didn't mean…" Gideon looked flustered. "Whatever." He gave a stiff wave and kept walking.

Now there's a nice view. Rowan chewed on his thumbnail as he appreciated the lines of Gideon's body. The man looked damn fine all dressed up, as always.

Had he ever seen Gideon in anything but a suit? A naughty image popped into his head, warping the true meaning of the question. *I meant something casual. Jeans. A T-shirt. Ugh.* He pushed away from the wall and followed the signs to the bathroom. *What was I even thinking? There is no way I should be leering after my boss, despite how fine he is.*

Advice Rowan clearly ignored when he ended up rescuing Gideon. At some point, Gideon had been coerced out of his seat by Paula, Adrian's mother, caught in a series of hugs and was manhandled into the center of the room. Like a bunny tormented by a predator, Gideon had looked helpless, and Rowan couldn't ignore the puppy-eye pleas to be rescued, cutting in to take his hand and lead him to the other side of the dance floor.

"You're really hating this aren't you?" Rowan pressed one palm to Gideon's waist and gently squeezed Gideon's hand with his other as they slowly turned in a circle on the dance floor. The day was almost over as they settled into the part where the songs slowed and those who made it through to the end came together as friends, family, couples to lock hands, hold shoulders, and say goodnight.

"Yes," Gideon uttered.

"I can hand you back to Paula if you prefer."

Panic widened Gideon's eyes. "Don't you dare. I'm ordering you to stay right here."

"Sure thing, boss."

Gideon turned his head, seemingly avoiding Rowan's gaze.

Ah, whatever. It had been interesting to see Gideon

flustered, a rare side of the usually serious and controlled man where his emotions were concerned.

"Stop smiling."

Rowan blinked. "Smiling? Who's smiling?"

"You. You're enjoying this way too much."

"I guess I am," he said. It had taken them a while to find any kind of rhythm together, and though it was nothing groundbreaking, the fact they could match one another and simply sway to the slow beat was enough.

Gideon side-eyed him. "Well, don't." He straightened, mistiming his footing and stepping on Rowan's toes. "Sorry. I'm bad at this."

Rowan chuckled, briefly pulling Gideon close. "Just relax. Loosen up." He pushed against Gideon's hip to encourage him to move, but Gideon gave him a blank look and seemed even more tense. "Never mind, this is good too."

Feedback whined briefly from the speakers, interrupting the fading melody as the DJ announced the last song for the evening, and suddenly Rowan found Gideon pulled from his arms. Darcy appeared between them, gripping their shoulders as they were brought into one large circle with whoever had remained until the end. He grinned as Darcy planted a wet kiss to the side of his face. He smelled of alcohol and sweat, but he looked beyond happy.

Darcy Bridges had tied the knot. Rowan never thought he'd see the day his friend would be so in love and equally loved. From the scrappy kindergartener to an awkward teen, through coming out, finding himself, choosing a career only to be forced to leave. Darcy had come a long way in those thirty years.

I guess we both have. Rowan's life had taken a few detours, but he was here, and he was content, and a large part of that was thanks to Gideon and him taking a chance on Rowan when he was at a low point. Leaning forward, he caught sight of Gideon, who appeared to have given in to the inevitable. Darcy had his arm around Gideon's shoulder, pulling him in tightly and Gideon smiled. An awkward but honest smile.

Rowan looked away as the same fluttering sensation from earlier warmed his chest. He didn't know if he could still blame the champagne from earlier, or maybe it was the fizzy soda this time, but whatever it was, he would cherish the moments he'd gotten to spend with Gideon. Tomorrow they would be back in the office.

And back to reality.

THREE

Rowan

"Ugh." Rowan groaned and pressed his forehead to the cool glass of the passenger door window. He and Gideon were in the back of a taxi headed for their hotel. "This is your fault," he grumbled.

"How so?" Gideon asked. His voice was calm, soothing.

"You didn't watch over your staff and stop them from drinking way too much. You're a sucky boss."

"If that's the case, should I expect your resignation letter on my desk tomorrow afternoon?" Gideon side-eyed him.

What is with him?

There was no expression on Gideon's face for Rowan to read and Rowan was irked. "You know, I'm starting to get the impression you're *actually* trying to get rid of me." He did his best to keep his tone light. He pressed his hand to his mouth when the back of his throat prickled from the burn of alcohol rising. Gideon didn't refute, and Rowan's heart clenched.

Alcohol had stirred his emotions, but not so much that he had no control over them. *Don't react. Don't. You'll just look like an idiot in the morning.*

Rowan lifted his head, slowly blinking. He eyed the blur of lights they passed. "Sleepy." Rowan slid sideways and leaned against Gideon.

"What are you—"

"I'm borrowing your shoulder until we get to the hotel."

Gideon sighed. "Seriously?"

He closed his eyes. "Think of it as making it up to me for all those times you fired me today."

"Want to be fired again?" Gideon asked.

"And rehired." Rowan smiled and relaxed a little. It was all a joke, right? Teasing? Gideon needed him. As a PA, as a friend, as…

"You're heavy," Gideon said but didn't push him away.

"Can't hear you. Sleeping." Rowan pressed his lips together, appreciating Gideon's warmth and his solid shoulder. If he wasn't careful, he would fall asleep for real.

They didn't speak again until they reached the hotel, Gideon stirring him from his shoulder as he leaned forward to pay.

Rowan breathed in deeply as he stepped out onto the sidewalk and looked up at the starry night sky. The weather had stayed fine all day and even now the December sky was clear, lit with starlight and the large moon.

"Rowan." Gideon was beside him.

Rowan looked at him and snorted.

"What?"

"No need for a bubble with a frowny face when you're already wearing one."

Gideon grabbed Rowan's arm when he swayed. "How were you on the dance floor until the end?" He sounded tired rather than annoyed.

"The trick is to never stop. You stop. You drop." Rowan scratched the back of his neck and squirmed to try to free himself from Gideon's hold. Gideon's hand was hot through Rowan's shirt, and the heat was spreading to places it shouldn't.

Ah. I'm getting horny.

He couldn't shake Gideon's hold, giving in with a sigh. He fished his wallet out of the back of his pants. "Keycard," he muttered and felt through the various slots.

"Do you want me—"

"Aha," Rowan declared and fought to free the plastic card.

Gideon shushed him.

Rowan pouted. What was he, a child to be scolded?

"Shush yourself." He chuckled and grabbed Gideon's loosened tie. Gideon looked good with his collar open, his waistcoat unbuttoned, his jacket over his other arm. There was an easiness about him as if he were just any normal person and it suited him.

A normal guy. A guy who isn't my boss.

"Come on." He tugged on Gideon's tie, toppled slightly, only to be supported by Gideon.

"Who's following whom exactly?"

"I guess I'll follow you. After all, you're the boss."

Gideon kept hold of Rowan as they went inside.

"A good boss." Rowan smiled. "I'd follow you forever," he uttered.

"Forever, huh?" They stopped at the elevators, and Gideon pressed the button more times than necessary. "That's quite the commitment." Gideon's gaze was on the counter above the elevator doors as the car made its way down to them.

Eventually, the doors opened with a clatter and the two of them entered. Rowan leaned in the corner and stared at his reflection in the mirrored panels.

I look like crap.

He closed his eyes and lowered his head, listening to his own breaths. Maybe he should have had more self-control with alcohol, but he had been swept up in the celebrations and forgotten who he was attending with. Despite both of them insisting they weren't boss and PA for the day. They were there as friends. Kind of.

Rowan cleared his throat as the doors opened and Gideon stepped out first.

"Your room is 314, isn't it?" Gideon said, following the signs.

"Yep." Rowan flipped the keycard over in his hand. "And you're in 330."

Gideon stopped when he reached Rowan's room, stood off to the side, making space for Rowan to get to the door.

Rowan slipped the card in the slot and pulled it out. He pushed the handle, but neither it nor the door budged. "Seriously?" He tried again. The lock made a small click and the light briefly flickered green but the door remained locked.

Is it me? Or the door?

"Let me try," Gideon offered, leaning closer to Rowan.

Rowan let out a startled sound as he caught his breath. Gideon was close, close enough for Rowan to feel the warmth from his body against his own.

"You're too impatient." Gideon slowly put the card in the slot then pulled it out. When the door opened at first go, he added, "There," and held the door until Rowan leaned against it enough to keep it open.

"Thanks," Rowan said.

I'm so embarrassed.

"Are you sure you're okay?" Gideon rested his hand on the wall beside the door and despite the route of escape into his room, Rowan felt crowded.

Is he doing this on purpose?

Rowan shook his head. "I'm fine. I'm fine." He blew out a breath then pressed the back of his hand to his mouth. "Nothing sleep won't cure."

He lifted his gaze. Gideon was looking at him with a serious expression.

"What?" Rowan asked.

"Nothing. Just wanted to see you to your room. Make sure you were all right."

He's being sweet. Too sweet.

Rowan chuckled. "Well, here it is. Or are you waiting for me to invite you in or something?"

"Of course not," Gideon insisted though Rowan

swore color flushed Gideon's cheeks as he averted his eyes and stared at the carpeted hallway.

Wait. What? What was that just now? Cute.

They stood in silence.

He's not leaving.

Rowan bit on his lip.

If he doesn't leave then I'll…

"Hey." Rowan gripped the bottom of Gideon's tie.

Gideon looked at him, and Rowan couldn't bear it any longer. He wanted to fill the moment, blow away the awkward tension.

"Rowan—"

Rowan arched his neck and pressed his mouth to Gideon's. He closed his eyes when Gideon pushed back against him.

This is…

Rowan leaned back and gripped the door handle to steady himself. He pressed his fingers to his lips.

What did I…? Why did I…?

He raised his head. Gideon was clearly unsettled.

Shit. Shit. Shit.

"Okay, wow. I am *so* sorry and *super* drunk," Rowan admitted.

I have to play this down. I'm an idiot. An actual idiot.

"I got caught up in the moment, Gideon. You know, all that wedding stuff. The lovey-dovey aura maybe rubbed off on me a little, and now it's just the two of us and the lingering. You were lingering and being all nice and concerned and…" Rowan couldn't stop waving his hand in front of him as he made excuses. "Maybe we should get coffee. No," he added quickly. "I meant to sober us up, not for…" He tilted his head. "You know. We, we, we're not like that so, not that I'm saying I wouldn't. I mean you're an attractive man and…hot, really hot, but…" He met Gideon's widening eyes that seemed to hold a burning plea for Rowan to *shut the hell up*. "Oh God, I should stop talking, shouldn't I?" He clamped his hand over his mouth, but all that did was remind him of the kiss, his lips on Gideon's or Gideon's lips on his or…*mutual blame*.

Gideon nodded. "Please."

Rowan swallowed hard. He'd messed up, and even if he was *maybe* drunk enough to forget what just happened by the morning, Gideon certainly was not. "Sorry," Rowan said quietly. He straightened Gideon's tie, patting his chest as he flattened the tie against the line of buttons of his shirt. "I'm really drunk. You know that, right?"

"Yes." Gideon's eyes shone with the usual comforting warmth.

"I'm not fired, right?"

"No."

"I should get to bed." He leaned against the door, pushing it farther open.

"We both should." Gideon closed his eyes and crinkled his nose. "You know I meant in separate beds, right?"

And it seemed with that the air about them thinned. Rowan snorted a laugh. Apparently, they were both idiots. He nodded and took a step backward across the threshold. "Night, boss."

Gideon closed his eyes. A slight smile, one of relief, curled the corner of his mouth. "Goodnight, Rowan."

Rowan closed the door and as if all his remaining strength left his body, he slid to the ground, his back pressed to the door as he rested his chin on his knees.

He loved his job. He loved working under Gideon. He was happy, content, challenged, and yet, for a split second, he'd given in to temptation. He came so close to upsetting his comfortable world. He could have ruined everything.

I'm never drinking again.

"Can I go home already?" Rowan mumbled against his desk to no one but himself.

The reality of last night's stupidity hit hard as had the hangover. The day had passed in a blur of paperwork and phone calls as he fought to secure bookings and deliveries in the increasing December panic as Christmas crept closer. And while Rowan silently went through several stages of a full-blown crisis about his actions yesterday, for Gideon it had been business as usual.

Had the alcohol god looked kindly upon him and Gideon had actually forgotten about his misguided affections? Unlikely. Luckily, for Rowan, Gideon was a far more put together adult and clearly had been able to move on, accepting the kiss as nothing but champagne induced insanity.

Kiss. Rowan's inner voice squealed in embarrassment. *We kissed.*

The wooden desk was cool pressed to his cheek, and he sighed as he stared at Gideon's office door, which was slightly ajar.

Gideon's so cool. Apparently, his inner voice was a high school teenager.

Huffing a breath, he sat up and pinched the bridge of his nose. Even though he hadn't come in until lunch he was exhausted. Yesterday's festivities, idiocy, and the early ride home had caught up to him. It was late and if he'd had any sense, he would have already been home, feet up, trashy soap opera on the television, eating chips and salsa, crashing on the couch in a pair of sweatpants. But no, it was almost eight in the evening, and he was still at his desk.

But that's because…

The main reason was to get a good week or two ahead of himself with work where possible before he took off for the holidays. There was also Jared, one of the employees whose popularity as a boyfriend for hire was almost on par with Darcy's. Jared's current client, some Manhattan socialite, had missed her appointment that morning and seemed to drop off the face of the planet for the day. Jared, always the professional, had struggled to hide the mix of irritation and concern in his voice, apparently wired on coffee having tried to work the problem himself. After all, Rowan had plenty on his plate already, and then there had been the wedding yesterday. Though Jared was being sweet and thoughtful, contacting Rowan earlier would have been for the best, giving him longer to track her down.

But I found her, eventually.

She had double booked. The meeting with Jared and a spa day with her girlfriends, and spa had won out. Despite the looming hangover, Rowan had been polite, cheerful, and after some shuffling on both their parts, rescheduled the appointment for three days' time.

A call would have been nice. He had dealt with many clients and businesses through Bryant & Waites. It would take a lot more than a missed meeting with a *boyfriend* to break his perfect PA demeanor.

He puffed his cheeks and blew out a breath, eyeing the soft glow inside Gideon's office. There was one more reason he was still at his desk.

Gideon. He'd been more serious than ever today, and Rowan got the impression it had nothing to do with the kiss. Gideon's expression when he thought Rowan wasn't looking was stern and thoughtful, his attention constantly stolen by his cell phone, his brow creasing in deep lines as if he was trying to solve a really difficult puzzle.

Nobody should have to think that hard.

A text message pinged Rowan's cell phone. With a heavy sigh, he checked the message. It was from one of his moms. He eyed the words on the screen, knew they were written out of love, but he couldn't help but feel slightly attacked.

Hi, Ro, hope D's wedding went ok. U can tell us all about it at Xmas. Thought u should know Ava is bringing her boyfriend this year. Remember there's always room for one more if u want to bring someone. We love you, Moms x

"Bring someone," he uttered to the empty space. He was thirty-seven, on the line between mid-thirties and late-thirties and apparently that was when he should be thinking of settling down, finding his forever-man, making a family of his own. He scratched the stubble on his jaw and thought maybe he should grow a beard like Gideon. He'd tried before, got to day four and gave up. Hell, he couldn't commit to growing a beard, let alone having a long-term relationship. Seeing Darcy and Adrian together, he'd admit he'd been a little jealous, but he wasn't sure that was him, not wedding bliss. Probably. And children? He loved family, the warmth of having people around him. His family were everything. But babies, little beings relying solely on him? He was not ready for that.

Maybe in a decade or two.

Even now, he didn't feel one hundred percent comfortable with who he was, and where he was in life. He needed to be sure of himself before adding people to the swing that was his life. He'd never stuck with anything for long and being at Bryant & Waites was the most stable and consistent his life had been in a long time.

If I haven't messed that up. If he fires me for real I have no one to blame but myself.

He thought about how his life had gone so far. Things would always end one of two ways, whether work or hobbies or men. He'd eventually hit a wall, either lose interest, become disillusioned, or conversely, be so invested, so passionate, he'd burn out.

Wow, that spiraled fast. I need sleep. He stared at the text, pondering his reply. His head hurt and he wasn't in the mood.

Wedding was great. And thanks. See you soon xx

Anything longer and he might come across as annoyed, which he kind of was.

"Whatever." He hit send, pocketed his phone then glanced back at Gideon's door. He was done. He wanted his couch, his baggy clothes, and his comfort food. He stretched his arms above his head and got to his feet, ambled toward the door, and wondered if he had enough energy to give a lively knock and bound in to say his goodnights.

No, I do not.

He stopped when he heard Gideon's voice. Was he still working?

"Mom, I'm really sorry."

A private conversation? Rowan pressed his hand to his stomach. He already felt guilty about overhearing part of the conversation Gideon had had with his sister while at the wedding.

"It's just busy here right now. No, no. That's ridiculous. I'm not seeing Dad. I'm not. Mom. Mom, I'm not lying." Gideon's voice was gravelly. He sounded tired. "It's work. So the only person I'll be seeing is my PA. Yes, Rowan. The one I told you about. No, he's not…Mom, he's just my PA. Yes." He cleared his throat. "Mark's son and his wife are still coming aren't they, with the kids? The new baby? There you go. You won't even notice I'm not there. You'll be cooing over the baby." His voice brightened a little. "Look, I should go. I'll stop by on New Year's. How's that sound? Okay. Good. Bye." There was a pause before Gideon said, "You can come in now."

Rowan sighed and pushed open the door. "That's kind of creepy, you know."

"Blame your shadow."

"Shadow?" Rowan glanced down at his feet. "Ah."

Gideon leaned back in his chair. "Did you need something? I thought you'd be home already. It's all you've talked about all day."

"Rude but accurate."

"So?" Gideon pressed.

Sliding his hand into his pants' pocket, Rowan gripped his phone. "I gather from the phone call you're making excuses not to go home for Christmas?"

Gideon shrugged. "Something like that. It's—"

"Complicated?"

"Yes."

"And the best you could come up was that you were working through Christmas with me?" Rowan quipped.

With a sigh, Gideon leaned his head back. "Yes." He seemed dejected.

"You lied to your mother."

"Yes. And my dad," Gideon added in a weary voice.

I don't like seeing him like this. There must be something I can do.

Rowan ran his thumb along the edge of his cell. What he was thinking in light of last night was probably ridiculous, and he would understand if Gideon shot him down instantly but…

I want to see him smile.

"In that case, let's do it."

"Do what?" Gideon questioned.

"Spend Christmas with me. Come home with me to Maine."

What am I doing?

Gideon rolled his head forward and wore a confused expression. "What?"

"That way it wouldn't be a lie."

"How much did you drink yesterday?" Gideon shook his head. "Because you must still be drunk."

"I'm not drunk. Not this time." He cleared his throat. "I'm serious." He stepped closer.

"I'm not doing that."

Ah. As I expected. But still, I don't like seeing him like this. I just need to give him a reason, right?

"Then, how about we make it a work thing so it's official?" Rowan countered.

Gideon was looking at him as if he was a mad man. "You want to take the accounts to Maine?"

"No." Rowan thought about the recent text message. *Bring someone.* "I want to take a friend, companion, whatever, home. I'll hire you to do it."

I am an actual mad man.

"So, how about it?" Rowan asked. "Let me hire you. For a discount of course."

Gideon laughed. "You're serious?"

"Yes." Rowan rested his hand on his hip. "You hate lying to them, don't you? This way you won't be lying."

"And you? Why do you need a *friend*?" Gideon continued his questions.

Rowan's heart clenched as Gideon emphasized the word. *Friends. Just friends. I want to keep working for him so that is all there can be between us.* But this wasn't just for Gideon. Nor for himself.

"Because it'll make my moms happy." He dropped his head and answered with heartfelt words. "And maybe they can stop worrying that I don't have friends in the city, and that I'm wasting away. I hate it, hate myself because I'm the one worrying them, and it's over something stupid, trivial, and untrue. They think I'm lonely."

In a soft tone, Gideon suggested, "There must be someone better suited for this. A real friend who could help you out?"

He's going to think I'm pathetic and lonely as well. But I'm not.

"To be honest, I don't have that many close friends. You know how it is, you grow up, do your own thing, meet other people. I would have asked Darcy, but he's a little busy this year, obvs." He laughed. "And before you have a pity party on my behalf, I am quite content with the socializing I do in this place to then go home and enjoy my own company."

Silence fell between them as Gideon seemed to scrutinize Rowan, his stance, his face. Was he searching for cracks? Wondering if Rowan's words were fake?

"Just as friends?" Gideon tapped his finger on his desk. "I don't have to—"

Please don't say anything about yesterday.

"No. No. God, no. Just be a friend. And if they suggest otherwise, tell them you're my boss, that should shut them up." *That's right, he's my boss. I don't want to lose my place at his side.* He put his hands together. *Who am I doing this for again? Gideon, my moms, myself?* "Please, will you help me out?" *This is such a flimsy plan. I say it's for me, for my moms, but I want to ease his mind, his guilt about lying to his family. He'll see right through me.*

"I guess it would mean I wasn't actually lying to my parents," Gideon thought out loud.

"Exactly."

And at the same time, I can ease my own guilt about the kiss. Let me make it up to you, let me share your burden.

Gideon huffed a defeated breath. "Fine. I'll do it."

"Excellent." Rowan perked up and turned on his heel to head for the door. "Oh, and just one more thing."

"What?"

"How are you with dogs?"

FOUR

Gideon

"Yes! Found it!" Rowan yelled and thumped his hand on the steering wheel, scaring the shit out of Gideon, who'd slipped into a state of hypnosis as he watched the road outside the window.

"Fuck!" Gideon yelped and clutched his chest before having to hold on for his life as Rowan made his way across the lanes to the exit.

They'd passed five burger chain outlets in the past hour, but none of them had been the perfect one according to Rowan. *Finally, he finds one and scares me to death? I knew we should have flown.*

His heart was still beating fast when they pulled into the parking lot and Rowan confidently backed into the furthest space from the restaurant as he could find.

"Are you okay?" Rowan asked and patted Gideon's arm as if he had absolutely nothing to worry about at all.

"You just…you…" Gideon thumbed behind them to the freeway, lost for words. His super organized, calm, efficient PA had morphed into something completely terrifying when he got behind the wheel of his beautiful Lotus. He was a good driver, but fast, and that didn't make the exiting of the freeway any less adrenaline inducing.

"I know. Cool driving, right?" Rowan said and pushed open his door, climbed out and disappeared for a moment before popping his head back in. "Coming?"

Gideon managed to get out, grabbing his coat and slipping it on before taking in his surroundings. This wasn't a chain outlet. It was a diner, a sparkling pink and white train car with a neon sign proclaiming it was Jen's Place.

There were so many questions Gideon wanted to ask at that moment. Why did Rowan have a cramped Lotus? Why was it canary yellow? Why did he drive on the edge of the speed limit the entire time and switch lanes so much? But mostly, why stop here at Jen's Place? He shut the door and took his time to get the questions in order. This morning Rowan had announced that they wouldn't be taking Gideon's BMW on the long drive up the coast to Maine.

His excuses ranged from that he loved driving to that it was his turn since Gideon drove to Darcy's wedding, and the fact he was hiring Gideon so therefore he was the boss, and Gideon should shut up and do as he was told. Particularly as it was snowing. Gideon had been too wrapped up in the reasoning to even question why the snow was an issue, but he got an answer for that as well. "I've been driving cars in the snow since I was ten," he'd announced and that had ended the conversation because Gideon didn't even want to know. "Things like that happen in a small town you know," he'd added as if that explained why he was driving at ten. How in the hell had ten-year-old Rowan even managed to reach the pedals?

When they left New York, there'd been a sprinkling of snow, a suggestion of a later storm, but the farther north they headed, hugging the ocean, there were fewer signs of snow, although it seemed just as cold to Gideon.

"Why Jen's Place?"

Rowan clapped his gloved hands together and huffed out an icy breath. "Kev was sick here," he said and then shook his head fondly. "Good times."

"Someone you know was sick in the diner?" Gideon stopped on the steps and gripped the railing, his glove sticking to the ice there.

"Uh-huh, Kevin, my big brother, the one with the… that's for later." He opened the door and a rush of warmth had Gideon instinctively stepping inside, unsure if he should walk straight back out as the gorgeous scent of burgers and bacon hit him. "It's my fault really. Mom was ill then so she and Momo stayed in the car with the babies and gave us the money for food. I dared Kevin to drink each flavor of milkshake, and he got halfway through and was so sick it was projectile—"

Gideon covered Rowan's mouth with his gloved hand. "No more."

Rowan wrinkled his nose and pulled back from the hand then shrugged off his coat and hung it on a hook.

"Hi," Rowan called to someone as Gideon hung his coat.

"Hey back, choose a table, honey, I'll be right over!" The waitress was old enough to be Gideon's grandma, steel hair short in a bob, laughter lines, and a ready smile. Her badge read Jen, but how likely was it that this diner, which seemed a relic of the fifties, actually belonged to Jen, this very waitress?

Rowan headed through the train car to the back corner, patting the vinyl topped table and then sliding into the booth.

"The family table," he murmured almost reverently.

"This isn't the one that Ken got sick all over?" Gideon looked at the immaculate area with a dubious eye.

"Kev, and no, I told you, it reached the—"

"Tell me something else about Kev?" Gideon was very good at changing the subject when it came to any and all explanations of childhood vomiting.

"The black sheep of the family," Rowan deadpanned. "Criminal record and everything." The waitress came over with water and menus.

"Back in a bit," she said and hummed to herself as she cleared the table across from them.

"What criminal record?"

Rowan blinked at him and then picked up the menu and hid behind it. "It's worse than mine," he admitted and glanced over the top of the menu briefly.

"Wait, what?"

Gideon knew enough about Rowan to have employed him.

At the interview he'd asked point blank about a criminal record with the addendum that hiring was based on his answer. "No, but my brother Kevin? He's the one you want to watch out for." That had been Rowan's answer, nothing about a criminal life that Rowan had somehow hidden because of course, Gideon had done a background check, which Rowan cleared with flying colors, and he'd assigned the name Kevin to the pile of things he didn't need worry about.

"Well, when I was ten, we borrowed a car. Legitimate borrowed," he added with passion as if that was vitally important. "Kev was driving, when suddenly, car met tree in spectacular fashion, and bam, one lengthy criminal record later…"

"How can you smile about that? In the interview, you told me that—".

"I'm teasing, jeez, you're not going to come over as a good friend if you freak out like that when I make a joke." Rowan shook his head as if he was disappointed in Gideon, but…what the hell?

Gideon very carefully laid his menu on the table. He already knew he wanted a burger, hold everything but ketchup, and fries and add the blackest of black coffees to the order. Anyway, he had questions now.

"Do you, Rowan Phillips, have a criminal record or not?"

"No." The *duh* on the end was implied. Where had his respectful PA gone?

"And your brother? Ken?"

"Kev. Kevin. No, not unless you can get arrested for projectile vomiting in an open space—"

Rowan was messing with his head, making jokes that weren't jokes, driving across multiple highway lanes to get burgers, and something was seriously off because Gideon couldn't handle it.

"Let's start this again. I'm here for the next four days, as a friend, and I have to get used to this new and frankly weird sense of humor of yours that is going straight over my head."

"What can I get you guys?" *Thank God for the waitress.*

"Thank you. I'll have a burger, plain, ketchup on the side, fries, and a black coffee," Gideon summarized, and she gave him a smile before turning to Rowan.

"Right," he said and sat back, patting his belly. "I'll take the Jen's special, add three onion rings, a spoon of extra relish, one pickle on the side, and I'd like an Oreo Christmas mint milkshake, a coffee, extra cream, and a side order of fries with cheese."

"Got it," she said and didn't comment once on that convoluted order.

He leaned forward as if he was sharing a secret, and Gideon couldn't help but lean in as well. "Last Christmas," Rowan faux whispered. "I stopped in and they'd run out of the relish. It wasn't the same. Summer before that, the A/C was on the fritz, but the burger they gave me," he smacked his lips, "it was intense and worth sitting in the heat to eat it."

"So this is a thing then, every time you go north you stop off here?" Gideon asked.

"Not every time." He lifted his T-shirt and patted his flat belly. Gideon refused to look. "Need to keep trim," he added. "Anyway, I thought I should show my *friend* the best spots between the Big Apple and Maine."

"We drove straight past Boston," Gideon pointed out.

"Boston doesn't have a Jen's Place."

That seemed to be conversation over. However, an awkward silence was something that Rowan never let happen in the office, and it appeared to be the same outside of that space as well.

"So, Kevin is the oldest of us. He's a lawyer, has a wife, Esther, and two kids. He went full white picket fence, apple pie life once he moved out." Rowan rested his chin in his hand and stared out the window.

Gideon tilted his head. Rowan had a weird expression, and he couldn't work out if Rowan was happy or sad talking about his foster brother.

"Then there would be Sarah and me. We're the same age, and Mom and Momo took us on at about the same time. Sarah's a beautician. Her partner is Jamie, and they are currently fostering twins, Bella and Jacob, whose birth mom must have had a thing for shifters."

"Huh?" Rowan did this all the time, threw in random things and then looked at Gideon expectantly as if he should know what Rowan meant.

"Go Team! Jacob? *Twilight*? Vampires?"

"Oh." Gideon knew about *Twilight*, had seen posters for the movies, and that was about the extent of his knowledge.

"And then there's Ava who, apparently, is *bringing* her boyfriend along with her this year, some guy named Lloyd." He quirked his eyebrow and pouted.

"Is that why—"

"Now I'm not judging but let's just say Ava can be a

bit loose and free when it comes to life and people." He bit his lip. "She dances at a club and is a terrible flirty drunk, so you should watch yourself." Rowan chuckled.

"And she'll be there at your moms' for Christmas?"

"Yes."

"With her *boyfriend*?"

"Once a flirt always a flirt."

Gideon sighed.

"Kevin and Sarah and their families will also be there."

"That's a lot of family." Gideon sat back in his seat and attempted to form a list that he could remember. Kevin, Sarah, and…*the dancer with the boyfriend*. Only Rowan wasn't letting up.

"It is. There were other kids over the years, some before us, some after, a lot of short-term foster placements. I've no idea where they are or what they're up to now. For us four, I guess we got lucky, or maybe not for someone looking in from the outside."

Gideon leaned forward in his seat as he listened.

"We didn't have places to go back to but instead we became a family. Moms adopted us." He smiled. "Speaking of which, I suppose I should add more names to the list you're trying to etch into your memory."

"I wasn't," Gideon bit back.

"I can hear those rusty cogs creaking. You should know my moms' names. There's Gill, Mom, and Jodie, who we kids all call Momo. I'm not giving anything away about them. You'll have to wait to meet them yourself."

So many names.

"They must be cool to have taken on so many kids."

"They have big hearts," Rowan confirmed.

Food arrived then, interrupting the conversation, and organized Rowan came back out to play. Everything on his plate and around him was laid out just so, and he realized Gideon was staring when he was about to take a bite of his burger, and he caught him.

"That's big," Gideon murmured, which was possibly the lamest thing he'd said all day.

Rowan winked. "I can take big," he deadpanned. Gideon spent the next ten minutes *not* staring at Rowan and concentrating on his own burger, feeling as if that had been an inappropriate exchange one minute and then wanting to snort with laughter the next.

Rowan confuses me.

But he'd never gotten close enough to colleagues to exchange sexually charged banter before, and he wasn't going to start now. He and Rowan were pretend friends, while being sort of real friends in a similar fashion so not everything was a lie. Finding Rowan cute or funny or being attracted to him in any way needed to be left at the door. Outside the door. Or in the next state.

Also, he was out of his depth here. He genuinely believed he could wing this as he did with any awkward situation, using a mix of politeness and having interesting subjects on hand to chat about. Only the closer they got to Rowan's home, the more nervous he was feeling. Rowan knew everything about Gideon, but it was debatable how much Gideon knew about his PA at all, other than the fact he was friends with Darcy, was ruthlessly organized, and had a family that would put the Waltons to shame.

They climbed back into the car and for the remainder of the journey, Gideon dozed off, his head against the window. Every so often waking to hear Rowan singing along to the radio or witnessing pockets of snow that dressed some trees in a dusting of white. Maine didn't always get snow, that much Gideon had researched so he could pack accordingly, but it was due this year for some, which would add to the Christmas spirit he guessed. If only he could chill, then maybe he'd have the first proper vacation since…he couldn't remember when.

"We're here." Rowan was excited, bouncing in his seat like a kid and then parking next to a beat-up jeep and whooping. "Let's go."

He couldn't see a house, just parking, trees, and an inch of snow until they rounded the corner and faced a stunning cabin of wood and glass, perched on a hill looking over a valley.

"My moms' place," Rowan said and pointed down the hill. "We'll have our own cabins down the hill. Look! The dogs know we're here!"

Two Border Collies jumped up at the gate seeming as if at any moment they were going to leap. One word from Rowan though, and they sat down, wagging their tails and wriggling with excitement.

I like dogs. I can handle dogs. But I'm glad Hilda could take Kimi in for a few days again.

"Left is Deon, right is Dog, the rest will be around in a moment."

Two more dogs came tumbling and chasing around the corner of the large cabin, sliding and piling to a halt next to Deon and Dog. One was big and shaggy, dark fur and bright eyes, and he parked his butt calmly at the back, but the other one, a tiny terrier, was all over the place.

"That's Bear at the back, and the little one is Widget."

"Bear, I'm gonna remember," Gideon admitted.

"Yeah, he's a Newfie. Sarah found him tied up and abandoned at the gate when he was a puppy, people around here know about the barn, and that we'd never turn away a dog and since our moms got a license for the dog fostering it's been mad."

"So wait, your moms now foster dogs?" *Instead of kids or as well as? How did I not know this?*

"Yep. They moved out here a year or so before I left home. There'd always been a dog or two in the family, but once they got out here, after some time and with all the space, they swapped angsty teenagers for troublesome pups."

"And these are rescue dogs?"

"No, these are family dogs. We just never seemed to find the right home for any of them, so they ended up staying."

Gideon glanced from dogs to cabin and back to Rowan. "All of them?" It was effort enough for him to look after a single cat.

Rowan shrugged in that 'what can I say' kind of way and then carefully unlocked the gate. "Sarah lives in town, and as I said she fosters now too, so she and the kids come and help out from time to time. Guess you could call the dogs therapy." He waved his hands to encourage the dogs to back up. "Stay," he ordered then held the gate open and ushered Gideon through.

Gideon regretted his life choices as he stepped inside. Wearing a suit seemed practical back in New York, after all, he wanted to make an impression, but now, with the dogs bouncing from paw to paw in anticipation, how long was his suit going to last? He braced himself for the onslaught of four dogs, but instead they bounced all over Rowan and didn't pay much attention to Gideon at all. The odd sniff, a gentle nudge to his leg, but this was calm.

"You can pet them," Rowan said, sinking to his knees right in front of Gideon, burying his face in one of the Collie's necks and gripping tight. "Deon is my dog. We all have one, all the kids."

The rest of what he was saying was a blur. All Gideon could think about was the graceful way that Rowan had sunk to the ground, his dark pants stark against the settling snow. And all he could think about was his buttoned-up PA falling to his knees and—

"Rowan! You made it!"

FIVE

Rowan

"Kevin, you're here already?" Rowan got to his feet, fussed over Deon as the dog continued to nudge his palm. "I know. I know," he said softly and scratched Deon's neck.

"Hey, Dog, come here." Kevin clapped his hands and crouched. The other Border Collie bounded over to him with Widget the terrier yapping as he chased behind.

"It really is called Dog," Gideon noted in a low voice.

"*She* really is. Kevin's eldest daughter named her. She must have been three at the time. Never could quite decide if Kevin was a genius or an idiot to go with it."

Gideon shuffled closer, his eyes never leaving the large Newfoundland. "It's kind of sweet, I guess."

Rowan narrowed his eyes. "Not sure your face agrees."

Gideon raised his hand to his mouth, a gravelly

sound catching in his throat as he complained, "Shut up."

Laughing, Rowan smoothed back Deon's fur. *Was I being sweet when I chose your name? Or being an idiot?* He froze as Deon made a gruff sound that rumbled against his fingertips. *Ah, I remember now.*

Deon had been a timid, wary puppy, unlike Dog who had instantly bonded with Kevin, like the balls of energy they both were. It had taken Rowan and the pup he was responsible for naming time to connect, and in some ways, it had reminded him of coming to work with Gideon. Having to learn each other's behavior, find a comfortable balance. "You were a grumpy little thing weren't you." He leaned down and stroked Deon, the dog flicking out its tongue and catching his chin.

He side-eyed Gideon. *I guess he hasn't noticed.* He couldn't help but smile.

"Do you need help bringing in your things?" Kevin called and made his way down from the main house. He was wearing jeans and a long-sleeve tee, the material slightly strained across his broad shoulders and muscular chest.

Looking good as always.

"Maybe later. We're going to go say hi to everyone first." He checked the gate to make sure it was closed. "Are Esther and the kids with you?"

"Nope. She took them to her folks for a couple of days, so they won't be joining us until tomorrow evening."

"Any of the others here yet?" Rowan enquired.

Kevin grinned and rested his hand on Rowan's

shoulder. His hand was warm, even through layers of clothing. *Always warm. Always kind. The best big brother.*

"Ava's here and settled in but I wouldn't rely on being able to talk to her. Sarah stopped by. Think she dropped off some food stuff for the dogs."

Rowan leaned his head slightly, wanting to close the gap. Even after all these years, his heart stirred a little in the presence of his foster brother. It wasn't so much romantic feelings as it was admiration, wanting to be doted on and protected, just like when they were kids.

"Hey," Kevin grumbled. Bear was jumping up his back, causing him to lose his balance. "You big dumb thing." He laughed and shuffled forward, bumping his shoulder to Rowan's chest as he tried to get away from the dog. "Big and dumb just like Sarah."

At over six feet, Sarah was indeed big, not so much dumb, though her ability to name pets was on the same level as a three-year-old.

But it looked like a bear when I saw it by the gate. I want to call it Bear.

Are we sure it isn't a bear? she'd joked.

"I'll tell her you said that."

Kevin laughed at Rowan and gently patted his cheek. "Come on. Mom baked." He flashed his teeth as he directed a wide smile in Gideon's direction. "You can introduce your *friend* while we eat." He walked to the house, with the dogs, except Deon, following excitedly behind.

With a sigh, Rowan closed his eyes and let the warmth of Deon's tongue on his hand soothe him. He hadn't seen Kevin since last Christmas. He hated it yet at the same time yearned for that feeling of being the little brother anytime Kevin was around. He had always looked up to him, envied his strength and his gentleness. Darcy had the same kind of aura.

Probably why I was drawn to him too. We weren't compatible though.

"What does he know?" Gideon's voice was close, leaving a trail of heated breath on Rowan's ear.

Rowan opened his eyes and turned his head. Gideon's face was next to his as he leaned into him.

So close.

"Know? Know what?" He looked over as Kevin stepped inside. *What was my face like just now?*

"About us."

"Us?" Rowan asked with confusion in his voice.

Gideon nudged his shoulder. "I don't want to sound like a dick so don't make me say it…I think he was looking at me funny. We're just friends, so what was with that big goofy face of his? That smile?"

Rowan laughed.

"It's not funny."

"Sorry. Sorry." Rowan patted Gideon's shoulder.

He's so cute when he gets flustered.

"As we agreed I told them you're a friend from work. That's all. You had no plans for Christmas and being so big-hearted, I took little old you in for the holidays."

"Little *old* me, huh."

"You know I don't mean that. You're not old. I mean, Kevin is your age, and I don't consider him old."

"Thanks. I think." Gideon bowed his head.

"Are you pouting?"

"No. You must think I am pathetic being alone for Christmas."

Huffing a breath, Rowan rested his hand on his hip. "Why would I think that?"

"I mean, it's an excuse, right? You saying you want to *hire* me as a friend for the holidays?"

I could shake you.

"Think what you like. As far as I'm concerned, you're doing me a favor," Rowan started. "Though, I won't deny that, like my moms, I can't ignore a stray. Especially the big adorable ones." He chuckled and lightly punched Gideon in the arm. "We should head in. We can get our things later when we head for the cabin."

"Yeah, about that." Gideon stopped him. "You said we were sharing but never really went into details."

"Oh, you mean the honeymoon cabin?"

"What?" Gideon's eyes widened.

"I…" Rowan started laughing and struggled to stop. "You are so funny. I'm kidding. But we will be sharing a room. Twin beds. Though if it's a problem I can sleep on a couch up at the house." He waved his finger over his chest. "Cross my heart."

They're going to eat him alive in there.

"You're the worst."

"Yes, yes." Rowan walked away, patting his leg, and called, "Come on, boy." He glanced up at Gideon. "You too."

"Ro…" Momo was standing in the entrance as he stepped inside, ready to scoop him into a tight embrace.

"Can't breathe," he said.

She eased her hold, and he relaxed into the hug. He breathed in the familiar comforting scent of her sweet perfume, baked goods, and dogs.

"Missed you," he uttered, burying his face in her shoulder.

Momo patted his back. "In that case, you should come home more often."

"I know." He hadn't been home since Mother's Day, having taken a few days' vacation.

"Though we do appreciate the calls every month." She released him and leaned back. "So, who do we have here? Gideon, is it?"

Rowan hooked Gideon's arm and dragged him forward. "Gideon, this is Momo or rather Jodie. Momo, this is Gideon."

"It's lovely to meet you," Gideon said and held out his hand.

Momo smiled but didn't take it straight away. "I'm sure Ro told you that I'm somewhat the hugger, so if you find that kind of thing uncomfortable, this is your one and only chance to speak up, and I promise to keep the hug harassment to a minimum."

"Earth to Gideon?" Rowan squeezed Gideon's arm.

He seemed taken aback, confused. "Sorry. I, erm, no, that's fine. Hugs are fine." He lowered his hand and despite his words, his body stiffened beside Rowan as he was pulled into an awkward one-armed hug by Momo.

"Well, it's lovely to meet you too. Feel free to call me Momo, but Jodie is just fine." She quirked an eyebrow as she patted his shoulder. "My you're a...solid young thing."

"Stop being a dirty old lady, or I'll tell Mom," Rowan warned.

Momo shrugged. "We've been together for nearly forty years. You think she doesn't let me look every now and again."

"Oh my God." Rowan pressed his hand to his forehead. *Why did I think bringing Gideon here was a good idea?* He lowered his hand in time to see Momo cupping her hands in front of her chest.

"Besides, even now Mom still has the best——"

"Oh wow, I'm parched. How about you, Gideon? Shall we get a drink?" Rowan tugged on Gideon's arm, making it a few steps when the one who he lovingly considered the Bringer of Chaos Number Two, Momo being Number One, emerged.

"Did someone say drink?" Ava leaned around the kitchen door. She held an empty wine glass loosely between her finger and thumb and was wearing a ruby-red hooded cardigan. The hood was pulled up, its thick fur trim framed her face, and stitched dog ears hung down either side, flopping and swaying as she ran in small steps and jumped at Rowan.

"Ro." She giggled and smushed her face to his before planting a sloppy kiss on his lips.

"Geez, you stink." Her perfume, mixed with the strong smell of alcohol, hit the back of his throat, and he honestly thought he was going to gag. "Are you drunk already?"

"It's Christmas," she slurred, her legs seeming to give out as Rowan was left supporting her weight.

"Geez. Momo?" He looked at her for help.

"Yes, yes." She hooked her hands under Ava's armpits. "At least let him get through the door properly."

"Boo," Ava said with a pout as she was pulled off him. "I want Ro. Ma bro. Bro-Ro." She snorted a laugh and squirmed free, finding her feet.

Rowan glanced over his shoulder at Gideon. Rowan wasn't sure he could describe Gideon's expression. Amazement, complete and utter disbelief. He was probably regretting agreeing to tag along. "She's not usually this bad. I swear."

"I've had my heart broken." Ava roughly prodded her chest. "Ow," she mumbled and rubbed the spot she had poked.

"Lloyd's an idiot. Rowan and I need to have a word with him." Kevin was behind her rubbing her head through the hood.

"We do?" Rowan remembered Lloyd was a bodybuilder type, built like an outhouse and fond of trying to lift Bear, or so he'd been told.

Kevin pulled Ava into a hug. "Gotta look after our little sis," he teased.

"I've got your back," Rowan said and then stepped back dramatically to hide behind the door.

"Whatever, little brother. Ava, come on, how about we get you some water and one of those cookies."

Ava curled down her bottom lip and sniffed. "Okay," she said, sounding small and pathetic.

Oh boy.

Rowan's family home was a far cry from the expensive sophistication of Gideon's offices, from his fancy suits and everything having its own place. In this family, organization was scored in the negatives then throw in some dogs, and it was a bubbling pot of emotions and insanity. But it was also a home of love and warmth and everything Rowan had needed growing up, and still did now.

In small doses. Very small doses.

"Are you okay?" Rowan asked Gideon. "I know you're here now, but if you wanted a timeout we can go and check out the cabin instead."

Gideon shook his head and pulled the scarf from around his neck. "No. It's fine. As you said, we're here so we should make the most of it." His gaze seemed different. *Brighter?*

"If you're sure." Rowan shrugged off his jacket and held out his hand to take Gideon's.

"I'm looking forward to it." A genuine smile spread across his face. "I'm sure we'll have fun."

"So, did you have fun?" Rowan asked as he dropped down on the bed. He stared at the ceiling light and listened to the sound of running water.

"I can't talk…just…give me a minute." He was in the bathroom cleaning vomit off his suit pants. Not his vomit, which kind of made things worse.

Rowan laid back and rested his arm over his face and grimaced. "Feel free to add it to your fee."

"I think I'm going to be sick." Gideon's voice was strained.

"Do you want me to do it?" He lowered his arm, glancing at the bathroom door.

"No."

Rowan sighed. "I thought you'd be used to things like this. You've cleaned up after Kimi before, right? She's a cat. They cough up all sorts, don't they?" He closed his eyes.

Gideon turned off the faucet. "It's not so much the sick as it is the volume." He huffed a breath as he came back into the room. "Was Ava okay?"

"Embarrassed mostly. Kevin was putting her to bed."

"Is she in a cabin too?"

Rowan breathed in deeply. "No, she'll have one of the spare rooms in the main house. Sarah and her kids will take the others. Kevin is in the next cabin ready for when Esther and his daughters arrive." Rowan licked his lips. "Ah, I'm withered."

"What?"

"Like a plant on a sunny day."

Gideon moved closer. "I get that. I guess your family is a bit like the sun."

"Yeah, hot and bothersome."

"I was thinking bright and warm."

Rowan opened his eyes as Gideon sat in the chair beside the bed. He held his suit pants in his arms, a dark patch up the legs where he had tried to clean them. Rowan's gaze drifted from Gideon's socks then up the dark hairs on his bare legs to the boxers showing beneath the bottom of his dress shirt.

"I'm really sorry," he said and looked away. "If you

want to go back, I'd understand. We might be able to get you a flight." He lifted his hips and fished his phone from his pocket. "I'll check for you."

"There's no need," Gideon insisted.

"Really?"

Gideon nodded. "I am rethinking my luggage, however."

"It's all suits, isn't it?" Rowan laughed.

"Not *all*."

"Well, lucky for you Kev is your size, and I'm sure we can find something for you to borrow if it comes down to it."

"I guess. But ignoring clothes for a moment. I'm not sure you've realized the more pressing matter at hand."

Pressing matter?

Rowan lifted his head. "What's wrong?"

Gideon folded his arms and gave him a firm look.

"What did I do?"

"Nothing."

"Then, what's the problem?"

Gideon leaned forward. "You're lying on it."

Puzzled, Rowan sat up. He examined the bed. A frown creased his brow. The only bed in the room. What happened to the twin beds?

It's a king.

Gideon

Gideon had seen this movie before. Steve Martin and John Candy sharing a bed in a hotel and waking up in a full-on man hug because they'd unconsciously sought out body warmth in the night.

Not happening.

Rowan stared down at the bed as if it was going to suddenly morph into two single queens, or maybe that a wall would sprout up in the middle. He was searching for solutions and Gideon had seen that look before when Rowan was doing the accounts and things didn't add up. The way he frowned, the way he stared as if by sheer will alone he could solve the puzzle.

"Oh," he finally said and scooted off the bed to stand by the side of it, arms crossed over his chest.

"I'm guessing you didn't realize this cabin had only one bed."

"I swear." Rowan held up his hands in innocence. "This used to be a twin cabin, and if I'd known it was one bed I would have spoken to my moms and reorganized." His lips twisted in a wry smile. "It will be cozy though." Rowan smirked.

"There is absolutely no way I'm sharing a bed with you."

"Settle down, I'll fix this." Rowan took out his cell phone. "Mom, small issue, this is one bed…yeah…no…he's definitely…no, Mom." At this point, he pushed a hand through his hair and turned his back on Gideon, lowering his voice as if no one would be able to hear him. "He's my boss, and a friend, not even a…Mom…didn't I tell you when I had Freddie over to sleep…yes I know you heard the banging…and Jeremy as well…but I told you…jeez…okay. Yeah, love you too." He sounded exasperated, but by the time he turned he'd schooled his expression into what Gideon liked to call client-mode. It was what he used at the moment he was showing new clients into the office. Official, calm, cool. "So," he began and then stopped.

"So?"

"Well, when I told my moms I was bringing a friend, and even with the backstory of you being alone on Christmas, which isn't a story but is the whole truth because you would be alone for Christmas, and I don't like—"

"Rowan! Focus."

"Sorry, it's just that they thought I was bringing a *friend*-friend."

"Huh."

He made a circle with his index finger and thumb then poked his other index finger into the hole. "Y'know, *friend*-friend."

Gideon rolled his eyes. He didn't need the graphics nor did he really want to hear about this Freddie or Jeremy that Rowan had clearly brought home and had sex with so loud his moms heard.

"So where are we sleeping?" The thought of sleeping in the same bed as Rowan and being drawn to him in sleep made him want to back the hell out of the door. Acting on inappropriate impulses that he couldn't or wouldn't carry through on, would ruin their relationship, could cause the company to implode, or worse, he might never see Rowan again.

"It's okay. It unzips, hang on." Rowan began rooting through the covers and pulled the pristine white quilt back until it hung off the end and then loosened the sheets at the corners revealing that the huge bed was actually two singles connected with a zipper which he tugged at.

"Uh oh," he murmured.

"Uh oh, what?" Gideon said and crossed his arms over his chest.

Rowan sat back on his heels. "Locked," he announced as if that made any difference.

"What? How do you lock a zipper?"

"I don't know, but it won't unzip."

"Let me have a look." Gideon crawled over the bed, getting caught in the bedclothes and cursing as he shook himself free. The zipper was there, the tab ready to pull, so he tugged it, expecting the teeth to open and for one bed to become two. Nothing happened. He tugged again, and then harder, but nothing shifted.

"Your thought bubble is pissed," Rowan observed

and drew a jagged shape in the air. "It's all, oh no I'm stuck in a cabin and I don't want to be here, and why is the zipper broken?"

Gideon ignored Rowan and his stupid thought bubbles. Getting a good hold of the tab he yanked hard, the tab snapped, and he went flying, backward, off the bed, and straight on the floor.

Momentarily dazed he looked up into Rowan's face as he leaned over the side of the bed and grinned at Gideon.

"Are you okay?" he asked and then bit his lip as if he was holding back laughter. *Asshole.*

Gideon stood and brushed himself down, taking care not to look at Rowan, who was flat on his back staring up at the ceiling. There was something about seeing Rowan laying there, a position he'd never seen his PA in before, that unsettled Gideon. Not that he hadn't imagined Rowan flat on his back in a bed, but that had been the first week he'd arrived at Bryant & Waites before he'd proven to be the best thing to happen to the company. Now Gideon made sure not to think about Rowan naked and waiting for him and in that way he kept himself in check.

"It's not going to unzip," Rowan said helpfully, and Gideon held himself back from snapping something sarcastic and on point. He was riled and didn't like looking stupid at any time, least of all in front of Rowan, who never messed up. "So who gets the chair?"

"I'll sleep in the goddamn chair," Gideon announced, opened his case, pulled out his travel bag, and then locked himself in the bathroom. If he left it long enough, then he had hope that Rowan would have remade the bed and gone to sleep. Was ten minutes enough? Should he shave or have a shower so it wasn't awkward that he was stuck in the bathroom for all this time? *Fuck's sake, I'm a grown man, what the hell am I doing?*

He brushed his teeth then realized he hadn't brought in the soft shorts he wore to bed. Hell, that was going to have to change because he'd have to add a T-shirt to that particular ensemble. It wasn't so much that he thought he would drive Rowan wild at the sight of his bare chest or be overcome at his soft belly but what if there was some accidental brushing as they passed each other and any part of Rowan touched any part of him.

Fuse lit. Bam.

Over.

Cautiously he opened the bathroom door. The bed was remade, and the covers were turned back on one side, but there was no sign of Rowan. It was only when he was fully inside that he spotted him curled up in the armchair in the corner, a blanket pulled up around his ears and two soft pillows behind his head.

"Please take the bed," Gideon said sounding more tired than he'd tried for.

"I'm okay in the chair."

"You can't sleep in the chair. Go back up to your moms' house."

"And walk in on whatever they're up to? I'm already scarred enough. You'd think at their age—"

"Take. The. Bed."

Rowan snuggled deeper, and his toes poked out from the blanket. "No, because it's a perfectly comfortable chair." This was clearly a lie as Rowan winced and shifted again.

"It doesn't look like it's the best place to sleep."

"So why are you demanding you sleep in it?"

"I'm not demanding anything," Gideon refuted.

"You're always demanding stuff. Do this, Rowan, do that, Rowan."

"Of course I do, you're my PA——"

"Do the other, Rowan, fetch me coffee, Rowan, sleep in the chair, Rowan."

"Wait, I never said you had to sleep in the chair——"

"Yes, you did. In your thought bubble."

"I don't have a freaking thought bubble," Gideon argued.

"You do, and right now it's a very angry and upset one, so I'm in the chair. You take the comfortable huge solid bed where you can sprawl out and sleep." He sniffed and brought the blanket higher. "I'll stay here, even if takes a while to sleep."

"Don't do me any favors——"

"It may take me some time but——"

"Jesus, Rowan, you sound like you're making a huge sacrifice like freaking Scott of the Antarctic when he went out of the tent."

"People get that wrong. It wasn't Scott. It was Lawrence Oates, and he was a hero. But then he was thirty-one so maybe with his younger bones, he would have been okay in this chair."

"Fuck," Gideon snapped. "Why do you turn everything into a circle of nonsense."

Rowan raised a single eyebrow then huffed. "If you

weren't so annoying I wouldn't have to." Then he closed his eyes, and hell, he thought he'd had the last word.

"You're fired."

Rowan snorted. "No, I'm not."

"I'm ordering you to get in the bed, Rowan."

Without opening his eyes, he shook his head again. "That's highly inappropriate from a boss to his PA," Rowan countered.

"For God's sake—"

"You're not sleeping in the chair, you'll put your back out."

"Rowan—"

"Gideon…" Rowan cut him off.

"You are possibly the most exasperating, frustrating, annoying—"

"Those are all the same thing," Rowan interrupted again and opened his eyes. "Your thought bubbles are tired, so go to sleep, Gideon."

Gideon made enough noise to wake the dead, pissed that he'd got himself riled up. No one except Rowan got him all messed up like that. Gideon took it out on his toiletry bag, his case, his shoes, all of his clothes, and deliberately took his shorts and a shirt into the bathroom to change, making noise in there as well.

I don't have a thought bubble right now. He was lying to himself. Then he went out, climbed into the comfortable bed, switched off the light, and pulled the covers up and over him. It was cold in the cabin, even with the heat on. Rowan must be really chilly.

"Do you want another blanket?" Gideon asked even though he'd promised he wouldn't talk anymore.

"I'm good."

Gideon rolled over on his side, facing the door, away from Rowan, and counted backward from a hundred. He only made it to thirty-seven and then gave up. He'd listened to Rowan move, heard the rustle of his blanket, and the squeak of the chair, and it was ridiculous that two grown men couldn't share a space as big as this bed.

"Rowan, get in the bed."

"Gideon—"

"We'll put pillows down the middle, we can share a damn bed." He sat up and switched on the light, just as Rowan clambered off the chair and stretched.

And there it was. Rowan in pajama bottoms, no shirt, his chest *right there*, his dusky nipples, the dark hair on his chest and then hair from the top of his pants, down…and *down*.

He brought the pillows with him seemingly unworried about his lack of shirt, or his stretching, or the way that Gideon got an eyeful of his PA's groin where the soft material draped. Rowan placed the pillows in the middle under the quilt and then reached for one of Gideon's and used it for himself before curling on his side away from Gideon, leaving only the very top of his head visible.

Gideon turned off the light and positioned himself so he was looking at the window and not Rowan. He tried to fall asleep, but Rowan had been right. Gideon did have a mess of thought bubbles.

I'm in the same bed as Rowan.

I'm hard.

And if Rowan notices, then I'm fucked.

SEVEN

Rowan

There was the sound of birds on the roof. Scratching, scraping, the noise of clawed feet overhead stirred Rowan awake. His head throbbed, his mouth was dry, and the taste of stale alcohol was on his tongue.

I only had two beers. Maybe rather than an alcohol-induced hangover it was the fallout from yesterday's adrenaline rush called family. Or the fact he had shared a bed for the night with his boss.

Ah, that really happened. Didn't it.

He hadn't fallen asleep easily. In the otherwise silent, darkened room, it was as if Rowan's senses had been suddenly heightened. Surrounded by the scent of home, Rowan could make out Gideon's cologne, mixing to become something more comfortable than he had ever imagined, and it unnerved him. Every sound Gideon made crept through Rowan's body and excited his imagination. He pictured Gideon's slightly parted lips as he listened to Gideon's steady breath and the occasional quiet sleepy sounds interrupting its rhythm. He remembered Gideon's legs, imagined them sliding over the mattress as the bed dipped and the bed sheets rustled when Gideon moved.

It really wasn't easy.

With a sigh, he opened his eyes.

Gideon. Rowan's eyes widened, and he jerked back. Gideon's face had been close. Too close. He studied his boss's features. Gentle yet strong. *Ah, my weakness.*

He rolled onto his back, hung his leg over the side of the bed, and stared up at the ceiling. What time was it? He arched his neck and reached for his phone, pawing at it until he managed to twist it so he could grab hold properly.

The brightness of the screen in the dim room made him squint. It was a little after seven.

"Too early," he uttered and rested his phone on his chest. Yawning, he considered what to do. He imagined his moms would already be awake. Even though there were no longer kids to rally for a school run, he imagined the dogs needed attention.

Rowan rolled his head as Gideon shifted beside him.

Is he awake?

Gideon curled up his legs, buried his chin in the barrier pillow as he mumbled in his sleep.

What was that? Luke? A name? Rowan tapped his fingers on the back of his cell phone and watched Gideon. *A dream maybe?* If it was, it must have been a good one. Gideon's expression was a peaceful one.

I shouldn't disturb him.

He couldn't remember the last time Gideon had taken any kind of significant leave or vacation time from the company, and every morning he would be in the office ahead of Rowan, waiting.

Another yawn made Rowan's eyes water, and he carefully sat up. "I am a ninja," he whispered to himself. "Maybe." The chances of him not disturbing Gideon were slim, but he took great effort to quietly move about the room, quickly washing his face, dressing, then slipping out of the cabin.

He winced as he pulled the door shut and was relieved to finally be outside. Operation Ninja had seemingly been a success.

There had been more snow overnight. "So now what?" he mumbled and turned his head, surprised to see Kevin standing outside the other cabin at the bottom of the hill.

"Morning," Kevin shouted. He tilted his head when Rowan quickly raised his finger to his lips. "What?" he mouthed and raised his shoulders.

Rowan cut across the snowy grass. There was a satisfying crunch beneath each step. He jogged to Kevin's side. "Hey," he said.

"Everything okay?" Kevin furrowed his brow.

"What? Oh, yes. I left Gideon sleeping so I didn't want your dumb loud voice waking him up after I took extra care in sneaking out."

Kevin laughed. "Why does that sound kinda sordid?"

Rowan pouted his lips. "Seriously?"

"Just saying." Kevin gave a smirk.

"Well, we're not all perverts like you." He pushed his hands in his coat pockets.

An amused expression passed over Kevin's face. "You forgetting that time I stopped by the old house? What were you? Fifteen?"

Rowan hunched his shoulders. "Don't remind me. That guy was a complete dick. As soon as he heard you inside the house, he jumped out the window. Just left me there."

"What would you have done if it had been Mom or Momo or one of the other kids?"

"I would have died of embarrassment." *Or maybe have run away from home.*

"I was traumatized. I have flashbacks any time I see a pair of stockings," Kevin said and stared off to the horizon. There was a smile on his face.

Rowan pressed a hand to his forehead. "It's not as if I like that kind of stuff. He just asked me to wear them and I thought…why not?" He huffed a breath. He'd had a hard time turning down people back then. Still did. Doing what people wanted was easier, would mean they'd stick around. Or so he had thought.

"That and bondage, huh?"

"It was his school tie. He went to that fancy private school." Rowan folded his arms across his chest. "He never did come back for it. Anyway, I'm not much into that kind of thing either."

Kevin shrugged. "I wouldn't judge if that was what you were into. We all have our kinks." He leaned his head and caught Rowan's eye with a playful expression.

"I don't want to know." Rowan shuddered. "Don't shatter my illusions."

"Fine, fine." Kevin chuckled. "Any plans for the

day?"

"I have no idea. Maybe help out around here. Maybe. I come home so I don't have to make plans, you know?" Here he wasn't ruled by his desk planner. However, including Gideon in his plan-less plans was creating sparks of anxiety. "How about you? Esther's arriving later?"

"Yeah, it'll be evening when she gets here. And as for me, I have presents to finish wrapping. But first I have a couple of errands to run in town." He curled down his lower lip. "The day before Christmas Eve, town is not my idea of fun."

"Christmas Eve, huh?" Rowan leaned his head. "I feel like I'm forgetting something."

"You've got my present, right?"

Rowan rolled his eyes. "Who said you were getting anything?" With a sigh, he added, "Yes, I've got your present."

"Oh good. I needed new socks."

"Shut up." He elbowed Kevin's side.

"Ow." Kevin sucked on his teeth then listed names. "…Ava, Deon, the other dogs? Do you still give Darcy anything? Who else is there? Or maybe it's something not present related? Did you forget your toothbrush? Need to go buy some new underwear? Did you turn off the stove before you left?" Kevin gripped the thumb on his other hand, wiggled it as if counting off ideas. "Something to do with work? Oh, Gideon, I didn't say him did I, or—"

"Ah, Gideon." He clasped his hands around Kevin's. "I need a favor."

I forgot. I completely forgot about Gideon's birthday. He'd been so focused on finishing the accounts, laying the foundation for jobs after the holidays, and then Christmas and family stuff that it had slipped his mind.

Kevin quirked his eyebrow. "What kind of favor?"

"Will you pick up a few things for me while you're in town?"

"Seriously? I was hoping I'd be done quickly. You know, in and out."

"Please?" Rowan begged.

Kevin's nose crinkled as he frowned. "Can't you go yourself?"

"I would but I'd feel bad leaving Gideon here alone."

"He'd be fine. He could keep Ava company."

Rowan gave Kevin a stern look.

"Good point," Kevin said.

"I'll pay you back. I'll do anything?"

"Anything?" Kevin grinned.

"Anything."

Kevin raised his other hand and flicked Rowan's forehead. "Idiot."

"Ow." Rowan let go and rubbed his brow.

"So, what do you want?" Kevin put his hands together and blew into them.

"Balloons."

"What?"

"Party hats. Streamers. Oh, a big badge with Birthday Boy on it and a card. Maybe one with cats on it." *The one I bought must have ended up somewhere out of sight, or I would have seen it when I packed.* "Wonder if Mom would bake a cake? Hmm, or should we buy one?" He looked at Kevin, who was wearing a disgusted expression.

"So it's Gideon's birthday." Kevin relaxed his shoulders. "Fine. You really want all that stuff?"

Rowan nodded. "Or is it too childish?" In seven years, he had never celebrated Gideon's birthday. It was on Christmas Eve, after all, they both were usually with their respective families or doing their own thing, so Rowan had never pressed Gideon about the day when he eventually found out the date.

"You know him better than me. What do you think he'd want?"

Rowan snorted. "He'd hate everything I just listed. Probably insist it wasn't his birthday and that the concept of celebrating is actually a myth." He only knew about it after catching the tail end of a conversation Gideon had been having with Kaden one time.

"Right." Kevin blinked. "So, what exactly do you want me to do?"

"Buy everything I just said and then anything else you think looks fun."

"You realize Esther is the one who usually does this sort of thing for our two?"

"Figures," Rowan said with a laugh.

Kevin made a strained sound. "Whatever. I'll do my best."

"Thank you. Oh, and can you keep it in your cabin until tomorrow?"

"Oh my God, Rowan." He rolled back his head and

flailed dramatically. "Of course. That's fine. For now, let's head up to the house. You can ask Mom about a cake or whether I have to try to find one of those as well. That *anything* of yours better be worth all this hassle."

He fell in behind Kevin. "You're the best."

"Yeah, yeah."

"Good morning, Gideon," Momo said loudly. She kicked Rowan's foot who was lying on the couch.

"Ouch," he mouthed.

Gideon leaned into the room, seeming hesitant. "Good morning. I knocked but…" He pointed his thumb over his shoulder in the direction of the front door.

"Don't be silly. Come and go as you please while you're with us." Momo was folding laundry.

Rowan wriggled higher to see Gideon better, leaning back over the arm of the couch. "Did you sleep okay?"

Gideon nodded. "Fine, thank you." Under his coat, he was wearing a light gray sweater over an open-collared dress shirt and suit pants.

"Rowan's been complaining all morning about the bed," she said with a grin.

"I haven't," Rowan protested.

She picked up the next towel off the clean laundry pile. "He has." She met Rowan's eyes. "You probably didn't pull the zipper hard enough. I'll have Kevin look at it when he gets back."

"No," Rowan said too quickly. "It's fine. I'll sleep here or something."

"Don't be stupid. Can't have you sleeping on the couch and scaring off Santa...or worse." She hummed what sounded like *I Saw Mommy Kissing Santa Claus.*

With a sigh, Rowan looked at Gideon. "Please, ignore her. In fact, ignore everybody. And you know what, ignore me too."

Gideon gave a low laugh. "Don't worry about it. We're adults. We were sharing a room anyway, so it isn't a big deal."

Rowan raised his eyebrow. That wasn't how he remembered the conversation going last night as they had argued over sleeping arrangements.

Ah, whatever. It was only for a few days.

Momo snapped her fingers at Gideon. "Oh, your pants. Did you want me to throw them in with the next load of laundry?"

"No, that's not necessary. I've bagged them up, and I can deal with it when I get home."

"You sure?"

Rowan shook his head. "Momo, they'll be dry clean only."

"Really? I could have sworn Sarah used to bring Jamie's suits over when we were doing her laundry for her."

"Maybe she did. Jamie's suits were probably..."— *cheap*—"...a different type."

"Oh. Well, if you're sure."

Gideon nodded. "Thank you though."

The room fell into silence, and Rowan felt awkward.

"Okay. I'm going to take the dogs for a walk." He got to his feet. "Come with me?" he asked Gideon and headed toward the entrance.

"Sure."

"Did you want any breakfast before you head out?" Momo called after them. "Need a coffee fix to start the day?"

"I already ate, but if you wanted something, Gideon," Rowan said.

Gideon shook his head. "I'm all right for now." He sat down and immediately Deon was up on the sofa next to him, his muzzle on Gideon's knee. Instinctively, Gideon was stroking Deon's head.

"He likes you." Rowan gestured.

"What's not to like?" Gideon smiled and then refocused on petting the Border Collie, who wriggled and rolled over for belly rubs. "I'm a likable guy," Gideon added.

Was he making a joke? Deon let out a soft whine when Gideon stopped petting him, and Rowan watched his buttoned-up boss immediately restart the stroking, much to Deon's delight. Any minute now Dog would be up on the sofa as well, the two of them were inseparable when it came to fussing.

As if he'd been called, Dog pounced on Deon, and both dogs ended up sprawled over Gideon. At first, it seemed like he didn't know what to do, which dog to focus on, but the dogs worked their magic, and then he was petting them both.

Momo walked over. "Oh look at you. They love you. Just to say Widget is upstairs with Ava at the moment, in case you think he's run off somewhere again."

"Does he do that a lot?" Gideon asked.

"Once the little shi—dog disappeared for three days only to be found sitting on the doorstep as if saying *where have you been?* when we came home one day," Momo recounted the story with a shake of her head.

"I swear you and Mom manage to keep the most troublesome dogs as part of the family." Rowan put on his coat.

"Could say that about some of the kids too," she said through a fond smile and rested her hand on her hip.

Rowan pulled on his boots. "Can't argue with that." He straightened, jumped on the spot, and flexed his toes inside his footwear. "Right, we won't be long." He leaned in and kissed Momo on the cheek.

"Have fun." She returned to her towel folding.

"We'll take the dogs on the land out back so they can run about. Means I can show you around the place while we're out there." He paused and sucked on his teeth. "Not that there's all that much to show." He waved his hands as if he was a tour guide. "And on your left, you'll see a fence. On your right, a tree. And what's this coming up, another tree. My favorite tree." He pulled open the door, Deon and Dog rolling off Gideon and leaving him covered in shed fur, not that Gideon seemed that fazed by his pants being covered in dog hair, but maybe he just hadn't spotted it yet.

"You have a favorite tree?" he said and stood.

"Actually, I do. There's this big apple tree near the

edge of the property. I find it pretty when it's in bloom, plus the apples are just at that right point between sweet and sharp in how they taste."

Gideon's expression softened as he smiled, coming to Rowan's side.

"What? Is having favorite trees too weird?"

"No. I was just thinking about how I couldn't wait to see it." His smile widened, and Rowan was mesmerized.

"Well, I doubt it's anything but twigs right now so…"

Gideon shrugged. "I would still like to see it."

Ah, what is this feeling? Rowan's chest tightened and there was heat in his cheeks. Was it because Gideon had genuinely taken an interest in something Rowan cared about? *Talking about trees. I'm so embarrassed.*

"Shall we go?" Gideon nudged his elbow. "Are you okay?"

"Yes. Sorry. I was thinking if there was anything more exciting to show you than trees and fences."

"I promise. I'm fine with trees and fences. So, lead the way." Lines creased the corners of Gideon's eyes as he encouraged Rowan.

Rowan's gaze was drawn to Gideon's lips. There was that smile again. Warm and honest. Pretty full lips drawing him in. He kind of wished he'd been drinking, so he could use drunkenness as an excuse to kiss him again. "Yeah." He turned away.

Where am I looking?

What am I thinking?

And why do I want to see his smile more than anything right now?

EIGHT

Gideon

At this moment all Gideon could think about was that he desperately needed trees, fences, open spaces, in fact, anywhere that wasn't inside and where he could clear his head.

He'd woken to the sounds of Rowan moving around the room, keeping his eyes shut tight, and waited until his non-ninja PA had shut the door behind him. Only then had Gideon turned on his back and stared up at the ceiling, wooden beams forming the cabin's frame. On a high shelf sat a painting of a lake, the kind that someone new to art who'd watched Bob Ross might try to emulate. Knowing Rowan's moms it was one of their kids who'd painted it and then handed it to them to be carefully framed and put in a position where everyone could see it.

What must it be like to have a family so invested in the creations of their children?

"Who knows?" Gideon had muttered to an empty room. He knew if he wasn't careful he'd slip into a pity party for one and reminisce on how his childhood hadn't been one where the refrigerator was covered in his attempts at art. Up and out of bed with his bare feet on the cool floor, he'd stretched tall and ambled into the bathroom. He hadn't looked at it carefully last night, but the shower was easily big enough for him. The water was hot, and on the plus side, there was a scented shower gel that reminded him of Rowan. Some small part of him felt as if he was taking a risk using it, for so many reasons, but when he squeezed some into his palms and washed, he closed his eyes and imagined that this shower was actually big enough for two.

He and someone else that he had no name for.

Not Rowan. Not at all.

Dressed, he'd gone to the house and heard stories about when Rowan was a kid, of Widget the dog doing something unspeakably cute that ended with Rowan laughing at the memory. Had two Border Collies sprawled over him demanding belly rubs and offering love and shedding hair in return. Then there was the awkwardness of Rowan having to insist that no, Gideon didn't need his suit cleaned.

Deon and Dog were now pushing them down the path, racing in circles as if they were herding sheep, yipping and rolling and then stopping at a small gate, with Dog clambering over Deon as if they were hugging.

"Look at that!" Gideon said, completely enamored with the fact that the two sheep herding dogs appeared to be best buddies and were hugging on their walk.

"They're inseparable," Rowan murmured and

whistled to get them to come to his side so he could open the gate, his gloved hand covered in crystals of snow.

He was walking next to Rowan in a few more inches of the white stuff that had fallen overnight. Gideon was in borrowed boots. His pants were tucked into them, and his hands pushed into the pockets of his thick jacket with his beanie pulled down to cover his ears. The one thing he liked most about snow was how it made everything so clean and beautiful, covering all the imperfections of the world, and even though the dogs raced around like mad things, the snow deadened the noise, and everything was peaceful.

"So this is it," Rowan said and stopped dead under the skeleton of a huge tree. With the blue sky, the white snow, and the ghostly tree, it was the perfect photo, and Gideon wished he'd remembered to bring his camera. Instead, he tugged his cell out from his pocket, caught an image of Deon and Dog hugging again before they darted away, and then took a couple of quick shots of the ghostly tree.

"Is that for your Instagram?"

He was confused. "I don't have Instagram."

"Yes, I know," Rowan snarked. "That was actually my indirect way of asking you why you were taking a photo."

"To show people, obviously." Gideon wasn't entirely sure who he'd be showing it to. Darcy probably. Gideon had thousands of photos in the cloud, but they were mostly for his viewing only. It wasn't so much sharing the photos as capturing something beautiful to remember. "Is this *your* tree?" He stepped forward and placed a hand on the solid trunk, staring up at the sky through the branches, then snapped another shot, but his gloves made it difficult to use the right setup for the photo on his iPhone, so he gave up after a while.

"Yep. This is the one. See here…" Rowan vanished into a large evergreen bush, and Gideon assumed he was meant to follow. There was a gap in the hedge that wasn't obvious unless you really looked, and he crouched a little to follow Rowan. The bush, whatever it was, formed an arch over them. They only went a little way in before the space fully opened, and the trunk of the tree was obvious. "It's a lot like a place I found when I first came to my newest foster house in the long list of foster families."

Rowan paused and now it was his turn to press a hand to the rough bark. "Back at the old house, when my moms first took me in, sometimes I needed my alone time. There was one place, with a tree and hedges, and there was a quiet space. I would hide away from the other foster kids when it got too loud."

"Peace and quiet is important," Gideon said because he couldn't think of anything better to say.

Rowan shot him a glance and continued. "With a book, cookies, and two cans of soda, plus a cushion and blankets, I would stay in there for hours. When we moved from that house to here, I was gutted that I'd lost that space, so I actually made this. I must have been sixteen, probably should have grown out of it, but I hadn't. Anyway, Momo and I hacked at this bush and made a corridor and dug over the ground. I didn't have much time to sit here, but she always said to me that it was enough to know I had it."

All kinds of emotion built up in Gideon at the mental picture Rowan was painting. He hadn't told that story to get pity or for Gideon to comment, it was just part of the fabric that made up Rowan, and he'd never hidden his backstory. He knew Rowan was adopted, but they'd never talked seriously about that before. He also knew he'd been a foster kid in a couple of places before landing with his moms. Rowan had never gone into serious detail. It was a dangerous line to cross. One minute Rowan would share memories of his childhood, and the next Gideon would be spilling all his secrets about his family, and worst of all losing Luke and how it changed him.

"Do you remember the interview?" he blurted and then wished he hadn't when Rowan looked at him curiously.

"For which client?"

"No, the interview for your position as my PA." He left the *duh* as implied.

"Oh." Rowan couldn't quite meet Gideon's gaze. "Yeah I do, sometimes when I'm lying in bed at night I'll think back on what I said to you about my adoption, and the family, and how it flooded out, and I get a flood of embarrassment at what happened. Not that I think about you in bed. Or…y'know." He waved his hand then led them back out of the way they'd come and Gideon wondered if that was the subject dropped. As soon as they were out though, Rowan continued. "I remember I told you my whole life story for absolutely no reason."

"It was when I asked you if you wanted a bottle of water."

"Don't blame me if I connected a bottle of water to my moms and the sad sorry tale of little Rowan. Anyway, in my defense it was the first interview for a position I really wanted, so a lot was riding on it, and you promised to forget what I'd said and not hold it against me." Rowan smiled at him because they both knew that Gideon didn't forget things in a hurry, and Gideon couldn't help but return the smile.

"I forget nothing," Gideon agreed.

Rowan huffed a laugh as they carried on down the hill to the bottom fence. "Don't I know it."

Deon raced diagonally from the far corner, frisbee in his mouth, snow kicking up after him, and Dog on his heels. A bit farther back was Bear, but he was lumbering at more speed than Gideon had expected from such a big dog. They were so free, lively, running, and jumping, and barking at the snow, and they were heading right for Rowan and Gideon. Not that Rowan noticed because he was busy chatting on about apple pie, or hedges, or something. Gideon wasn't listening. He was abruptly filled with concern as he focused in on the running dogs. Any minute now they were sure to turn, and right on cue Deon swerved, and Dog followed. But at the moment Gideon relaxed, Bear had no brakes or the ability to swerve. Missing Rowan by an inch and barreling into Gideon at full speed, taking his legs out from under him and sending him tumbling into the snow.

His breath left him in a sudden whoosh, there was chaos and barking, and he closed his eyes as he was licked and loved and not by Rowan, but by a one hundred forty pound Newfoundland.

"Bear! Get. Off," Rowan shouted, at least it sounded like Rowan, who else would it be. *Why is everything upside down?* Finally, Bear was off him, and instead of a dog, it was Rowan's beautiful melted chocolate gaze that Gideon focused in on. "Jeez, Gids, are you okay?"

"Gah," was all Gideon could manage—he couldn't even correct Rowan shortening his name. Rowan must have taken his gloves off because his hands were hot as they cradled Gideon's face, and the shock of having Rowan's hands on him was doing nothing for his equilibrium.

"Hey, can you stand, should I call 911? Fuck it, I'm calling 911. Bear took you out like a bus—"

Gideon gripped Rowan's hand. He wasn't hurt. He was breathless, and he'd probably ache in a few hours, but the last thing he wanted to do was get trapped in the ER for a single moment of his Christmas break. He would endure family, and eggnog, and gifting presents, and fun, and kids, and dogs, if it meant no to a hospital bed.

"No 911," he muttered and then rolled onto his belly, thinking that maybe he'd get a better start at standing up. Then he was on all fours, and Rowan was *right there*, behind him, wrapping arms around him and helping him to stand. Sue him if he leaned on Rowan more than he needed, but damn the man smelled good, and the snow was cold, and he felt weird and out of place. Rowan was strong—easily holding him up— which was a really nice feeling. He sometimes forgot that Rowan was a man and could easily bench press whatever weight it was that was good to bench press. Not that Gideon knew much about that, but somehow in this single moment Rowan wasn't a PA...he was a man.

All man. Sexy and strong and caring and holding me upright.

A dog barked, more of a yip than a woof, and other barks joined the chorus. Rowan tried to quiet them, fear in his tone, and then Ava's voice joined in the melee.

"What the hell?"

"Bear took him out in one strike."

"Did you call 911?"

"No 911. Jeez, I'm okay," Gideon protested, pulling away from Rowan and dusting himself down, hot with embarrassment. "Let's keep walking."

Rowan poked at his arm. "You're sure?"

"I didn't hit my head. I feel fine, and we need to... dogs...walk." He waved his hand at the nearest dog, Deon, who was staring up at him as if he had two heads, or maybe silently judging Gideon for not getting out of the way for Bear. He could imagine dog-speak where he was the idiot and the dogs were laughing at him.

Did I hit my head? Or am I just losing my shit?

Deon and Dog settled in right next to Gideon as if they were protecting him, and just like that they finished the walk, talking about snow, and Christmas, or rather Rowan and his sister were chatting about that, Gideon just listened. Rowan's voice wasn't *Rowan*. He was edgy, too bright, clearly worried about Gideon. Rowan would stop talking every so often to check on him. Rowan was worse than one of his Collies as he herded Gideon back to the house. The reason why he was so intent on getting back to the house became obvious as soon as they got inside.

"Mom, Bear wiped Gids out!" Rowan guided Gideon to the kitchen and made him sit on a chair. "Mom knows first aid."

"I know first aid," Gideon protested.

"Oh goodness." Gill appeared at the kitchen door and just as quickly disappeared the way she came, only to pop up shortly after with a huge box. She laid it on the table and opened it. Inside was everything from bandages to Band-Aids to cough syrup to…wait, was that needles?

"I'm fine—"

"Hold still and let me look." She tilted his chin, shone a light in his eyes, and checked his pulse. "I remember Bear sitting on me when he was only a year old, he's a huge bundle of love and weight all rolled into one. Now does anything else hurt? Are you in any pain?"

"No. Thank you."

She startled the hell out of Gideon when she pressed a kiss to the top of his head, but then she leaped back in horror.

"Oh my God, I'm sorry. I'm so used to kissing the booboos better with all the kids that…"

"No, don't be sorry." He wasn't going to go as far as

to say that it was a good feeling to have the mom-kiss from Gill, something he sorely lacked in his own upbringing. But Ava holding onto Bear as if the dog was going to launch himself at Gideon again, now that felt nice. Not to mention Rowan was standing so close that Gideon could feel his body warmth. He didn't need to be protected. He could look after himself. But this family was cocooning him, and it felt so weirdly good.

He took his Advil as instructed by Gill and iced his knee. He only ached a little by the time dinner came and went and felt positively lighter in his heart by the end of the night. Deon hadn't left his side, not just demanding belly rubs but resting his head on Gideon's lap. He was the best of good dogs, and Gideon's fingers were tired from belly rubs. Tonight he'd met siblings and their kids. It was loud, chaotic, and funny, and he'd had a good time. Everyone seemed caring. The kids asked him about his knee, and one of them, Clara he thought, drew a picture of him with a crutch, at least that is what she said it was. Then there was Rowan—seeing him like this was a revelation. At work, he could be sarcastic, bordering on disrespectful as a PA, but he could turn it off in an instant to be effortlessly professional with clients. Gideon never told him how much he loved that disrespectful side, those times that Rowan pushed Gideon to the edge before smiling and yanking him back. Gideon would never admit how much he loved having Rowan as a PA. Without Rowan, Gideon's workspace would be a dark and officious place with no laughter or teasing.

Here with his family, Rowan was funny, and every so

often he would slip and call Gideon Gids or lean on him whenever he made a joke. It was telling that Gideon didn't correct him once. Rowan was chilled and excited to be home, and it was a new side to Rowan that Gideon was growing to love. By the time the two of them arrived back to the cabin Gideon was mellow from the company, but he knew for sure that tonight it would be a lot easier to sleep in that same bed. Because now he'd seen Rowan like this, he knew even more that he wanted to keep him as his PA. He *needed* Rowan in his life, to keep him from fucking up and to keep him sane, and there was no way he was messing that up by fooling around and acting on the lust growing inside. He just had to ignore the fact he had a hard-on at the thought of being in the same bed as Rowan. Easy. They could be grownups about this, and he didn't have to recall the warmth of Rowan's hands on him in the snow, or the way in the middle of last night Rowan had rolled into the middle, the barrier of pillows meaning nothing as he had half-spooned Gideon from behind. That would never be talked about.

Gideon was never going to act on any kind of attraction.

Ever.

So why was it such a crushing blow to step inside the cabin, only to find that someone had separated the two beds into singles, with a cabinet between them?

NINE

Rowan

With a groan, Rowan sat up in bed. Somehow, he'd had a worse night's sleep than the last. He wasn't sure why, but he'd found himself even more aware of Gideon than before, despite being in separate beds.

A bang in the bathroom drew his attention. "You okay?" he called and scraped back his hair. There was no answer. "Gideon?"

"I'm fine. Just dropped the…thing," Gideon called back, his answer muffled slightly by the sound of the shower.

"Need a hand?" Rowan asked. He drew up his legs and rested his chin on his knees. "Just kidding," he added for himself.

"I'm fine," Gideon said for a second time.

Was he really?

He hadn't said anything, but it was easy to see Gideon's knee was a little swollen and the faint glow of a bruise was forming, and though he had faced the morning as normal, it seemed his stoicism was slipping.

Soft grunts had escaped from his tight lips when he got to his feet and moved about.

Maybe I should cancel the plans for today? It wasn't as if he'd arranged something particularly special for Gideon's birthday and there'd be the usual Christmas Eve drinks and snacks later that evening, but still, people had put in the effort. It would be sad to see them go to waste. *I'll ask them what they think.*

He rested his forehead on his crossed arms, closed his eyes, and listened to the sound of running water. It was strange. His mind filled with Gideon. Rowan had always considered him to be attractive. Gideon, on the surface, was everything he wanted in a lover—mature, strong, kind. Rowan had always avoided coming across as needy, put up the façade that he was fine by himself— and he was. He wasn't a useless person, his job as PA proved it.

Proved it to whom exactly?

To himself? To those he thought might abandon him when he was no longer useful to them?

What am I thinking about?

His childhood anxieties reared in his chest. Ached.

Haven't felt like this in a while.

He gently stroked his chest with the back of his hand. When he was a child, about five years old, his real mom left him alone. Sometimes he wished she'd been a terrible mother, but in the end, she'd just been ordinary. A regular, flawed human being. His father had died when he was a baby and Rowan, from the bits he remembered, didn't feel his childhood had been anything but normal, or at least until that one day when his mother came to his bedside, told him to be a good boy, and that she would be back soon. Soon, however, turned into days then into almost two weeks. When she did show up, neighbors had already called social services. He didn't remember much else from back then, but the look of relief on her face was forever burned into his memories. He'd reached out to her, but she never took his hand. She let him go.

Rowan breathed in deeply and lifted his head when the water shut off. Obsession or indifference. He was a people pleaser who went all out or someone who kept people at a distance. For the longest time he thought why put the effort into something that would come to an end eventually? His life swung in one direction or the other. It wasn't until working at Bryant & Waites, he found himself capable of walking the line between the two.

What about the job had caught his interest?

It was certainly a tangent to his time working in the pharmaceutical industry. Several years ago, he'd taken a timeout, traveled around India, hoped for the brochure-type promise of finding himself, finding a direction. Maybe become one with the earth, find love for his fellow man, some inner peace, try meditation, be Zen or whatever was fashionable back then. In the end, all he'd wanted was for something to change. In a way, it did, but not for him, not directly, but for Darcy instead, and while Rowan had chosen to leave his career, Darcy was forced from his, and his thoughts were shifted from himself to his friend.

On returning to New York, Rowan took a chance,

applied for the PA position, and even surprised himself with how diligently he took to the role. Was it Gideon's influence? Or maybe Darcy's new circumstance had finally made him realize something about himself? Whatever the reason, for the first time in his adult life, Rowan was content, comfortable, but also strove to do his best, to properly be part of something.

And in the end, I even roped Darcy into working there.

"Are you all right?" Gideon was standing beside his bed, a large bath towel wrapped around his waist, coming just below his knees. He brushed back his wet hair. Droplets ran down his cheeks and fell over his shoulders and chest.

Broad shoulders. Nice skin. Twin moles on his collarbone.

Rowan smiled. "Yep. I'm fine. Are you? Did the warm water help?"

Gideon sat on the end of the bed and winced. "A little." He leaned forward and pulled up the towel. "Looks worse than it is." His cheek twitched. "Well, maybe." He chuckled and leaned back, holding himself up on his arms. "I guess Bear lives up to his name."

"Yeah, sorry."

"It's not your fault." Gideon yawned.

"Tired?"

"Mmm. A little."

Rowan eyed Gideon's upper body. What would it feel like holding that body to his own? Firm in parts, soft in others. The feel of hot smooth skin and his fingertips running through the patch of chest hair. What was Gideon like in bed? What position did he prefer? Rowan was used to taking on whatever role his partners desired.

You should be a little more selfish. Who had told him that?

If I was to be selfish? He chewed on his fingernail. *I'd probably want to top. Have Gideon hold onto me, wearing a desperate expression.* Though the opposite was just as an enticing image, and if he was being honest, his imagination had, at times, wandered in that particular direction while at the office—Gideon pressing him up against the filing cabinets, having him straddle him in his chair, or taking him over his desk, papers scattering everywhere.

Yeah, I could go for that too.

Rowan lifted his hips. His thoughts were affecting his lower half. He squeezed his legs together.

But if he was truly being selfish, then it would be to stay at Gideon's side, and the best way to do that was as boss and PA.

Wasn't it?

Rowan dragged himself to the edge of the bed, grateful for the baggy pajama bottoms. "Shower," he said and headed to the bathroom.

"Sure," Gideon said as he passed.

Rowan locked the door then stood over the sink. He gripped the edge of the basin with one hand and pressed his other palm to his erection.

"I'm an idiot."

He stripped and stepped into the shower, hoping the water was enough to muffle the sound of him jerking off.

Idiot.

"Here. It's blueberry."

Gideon stared at the muffin. "It's warm."

"Freshly baked." Rowan smiled and dropped down in the chair beside the bed. "Do you feel up for an adventure this afternoon?"

Gideon folded down the napkin and cupped the muffin in his hands. "Depends on the adventure."

It was now after lunch. Gideon had stayed in the cabin for the morning with his leg up on the bed, resting his aching body away from the chaos that was already unraveling in the main house. Kevin's kids and the family dogs had worked each other up into a bouncing ball of Christmas excitement.

"A drive. Thought I could live out my dream of being a tour guide and point at things, tell amusing anecdotes as we cruise on past." He shrugged. "Only if you want to. If you'd prefer you can stay here and rest, prepare yourself for later. This evening will be a bit hectic since Kevin's wife and kids are here, and later Sarah and her family will be showing up and staying over."

As much as Rowan loved the idea of hiding out here in the cabin with Gideon, it was Christmas and this was his family. He had no intention of skipping out on them. But this was a chance of a little bit of quiet time, just the two of them. It would also give the rest of the family a chance to finish setting up for Gideon's birthday surprise.

Surprise? A bunch of balloons and a cake, was that much of a surprise?

"…wan. Rowan."

"Huh? Oh, sorry. What?"

"I said a drive sounds good."

"Great. I'll tell Mom we're taking the van."

Gideon raised an eyebrow.

"Or do you want to be squashed in the Lotus with your knee like that?"

"Ah." Gideon lowered his head and smiled. "You're always thinking ahead."

Rowan jumped to his feet. "Part of my job after all. Okay, eat up and get ready. I'll head over and tell everyone our plans."

Ten minutes or so later they were in the large van. Rowan settled behind the wheel, and the passenger seat pushed back as far as it could go to leave space for Gideon to stretch his legs, with snacks on the back seat.

"Right." He wiggled his butt in the seat, checked the distance to the pedals, and touched the mirror. "Been a while since I drove this thing." He glanced over at Gideon whose brow furrowed. "Relax. It'll be fine."

"You say that, but I never did hear the whole story about you or Kevin or whoever crashed a car."

"It was Kevin, and it was the family car. We were supposed to just be sitting in it as it warmed up before Momo came out to clear the ice off the windshield."

"Supposed to?"

"We were kids and Kevin liked showing off so he was pretending to drive but…he ended up releasing the handbrake. The car was on a slope so…"

"So, what?"

"The car rolled down the slope. Kevin panicked and couldn't find the brake pedal. I thought it was cool because Kevin looked as if he was properly driving, and we hit the tree on the opposite side of the street."

"Wow," Gideon said.

"Not what Momo said."

Gideon cleared his throat with a laugh. "I bet."

"Anyway." Rowan gripped the steering wheel. "Ready?"

Gideon rested his elbow on the door. "As I'll ever be."

"Meanie," Rowan uttered through a grin.

The drive was filled with comfortable, meaningless conversation, mostly about other playful escapades of Kevin and the other children.

"The Ewok? She really thought it was called Widget?" Gideon laughed.

"The guy she was dating at the time was a big *Star Wars* fan, and she embraced her inner geek for a while. It was probably more for show to impress him, so I think she'd only watched the movie once. Ava had been calling the dog Widget for weeks before anyone corrected her. In the end, it was for the best. He dumped her the following month." Rowan turned his head, searching for a place to park. "She really does have no luck at all when it comes to men…" he trailed off as he focused his attention and pulled into the roadside space and straightened the vehicle.

"Here we are. You up for a short walk? Thought we could get some ocean air."

"I can manage for a while." Gideon opened his door and got out onto the sidewalk with a small grunt. "Cold," he muttered and pulled his coat more tightly about him.

"It's sheltered a little up ahead, there's a bench." He leaned into the back and grabbed a Tupperware container. "Do you want to borrow some gloves? I brought a spare pair." He tucked his scarf in his jacket and pulled the zipper higher then got out.

Gideon shook his head, fishing a pair of his own from his coat pockets. "I'm fine."

Rowan locked up and walked around the van to join Gideon. He briefly hugged Gideon's arm, squeezing him tightly. "Come on," he said and tugged at his sleeve before letting go.

The viewing area was a few minutes from where they had parked, backed by hedges and surrounded by plants that dulled the briskness of the salty air blowing in over the ocean.

Rowan sat and brushed the seat beside him while Gideon arranged the bottom of his coat.

With a sigh, Gideon joined him. "Cold," Gideon said for a second time.

Rowan laughed and rested his hands on the plastic tub.

"What's in the box?"

"Oh, something." He was vague, and Rowan could tell that Gideon really wanted to ask for more information. "There's a bakery not far from here. Our moms would buy us pastries when we were kids, and we'd come up here to eat them."

"So it's a pastry."

"Yeah." He looked out at the rolling waves, lost in memories.

"Do you like coming to the ocean?" Gideon asked gently.

Rowan shrugged. "I don't mind it. I think it's more the family memories I appreciate about the place rather than the ocean itself."

"Your family means a lot to you doesn't it?" There was something solemn, lonely in Gideon's words.

"They do." He nudged Gideon's arm. "My friends too. Hired or otherwise."

"You're still saying that?"

Rowan smiled. "I didn't want to be presumptuous. I mean you're my boss first, and I'm your PA." He looked at Gideon, meeting his dark gaze. "But if it's okay with you, I wouldn't mind calling you a friend."

Gideon turned to look at the horizon. "I think that's fine. If I can do the same."

"For you," Rowan said and pushed the tub against Gideon's chest.

Gideon tilted his head. "Me?"

"Just take it."

Gideon took the tub and narrowed his eyes.

"As I was saying, there's a bakery, but I wasn't sure if it would be open what with it being Christmas Eve today, so this is the best I could do. Or rather Mom did because I can't bake to save my life. She made a batch for breakfast. But I did do the icing."

"Okay." Gideon removed the lid and carefully folded back the napkin. "This is…"

"Happy Birthday." Rowan jumped in and waved his hands. "Yeah, about the icing. It was a bit fiddly trying to spell it all out on there, so it reads more like Hoppy Birthday Gidoon. But it's the thought—"

"Thank you," Gideon interrupted. He stared down at the cinnamon roll. "I didn't realize you knew."

"Well, yeah, I know a lot about you, but Christmas is a busy time usually and not being at the office means it slips past. I feel bad I never said anything but thought since this time we're together, and well—" He shut up when Gideon grabbed his hand.

"I mean it. Thank you." Gideon's gaze was intense, and Rowan thought he would have melted to the ground if he'd been standing as a warm sensation spread from his chest down to his knees.

Gideon gripped his hand and wasn't letting go.

Rowan turned his hand over and squeezed back. He didn't understand Gideon's reaction to such a small gesture, but he was glad it had made Gideon smile.

They sat quietly together, and Rowan watched the waves against the shore.

Please let us stay like this for a while. Please.

TEN

Gideon

Why did I hold his hand? Was it because he gave me a pastry?

All Gideon could think about was that holding hands felt right, but at the same time it could be a step too far in their business relationship. His brain went into overdrive attempting to rationalize what was happening.

It's just a pastry.

The iced cinnamon roll was the only thing he could think about. He couldn't actually recall the last time he'd had anything this thoughtful, be it cake, or in this case a pastry, on his birthday.

"Kaden and I just text each other on our birthdays," Gideon heard himself say, the words pulled from deep inside him.

"June seventeenth," Rowan said. "He's a Gemini."

"Do you believe in all that?"

"Not really, I mean, I'm a Virgo which allegedly makes me neat and obsessively worried over details. Outside of work, details slip because I think I don't want to know what is coming next."

"But you know Kaden's birthday?" Gideon asked.

"He's your cousin. He works for us, and I like birthdays."

"We don't exchange gifts."

Rowan nodded. "You'd be all worried about getting the right one, and that concern equates to angst over missed posting dates and the appropriateness of said card. Plus, you'd stress over what you'd give him as a gift, just like you did the wedding present."

That was so spot-on that Gideon winced. "I wouldn't know what to get him. He was already fifteen when he turned up in my life, and I was thirty. We were at different times in our lives. Way back, I didn't want to embarrass myself by buying something stupid for him, so I told him it was okay not to worry about birthdays."

"What about your sister Grace? What do you do with her for birthdays?" Rowan questioned.

"Not much, it's bad timing that mine is Christmas Eve, y'know? So she doesn't get me anything, or maybe she rolls it together with a Christmas gift, but mostly we decided my birthday was inconvenient, so we decided to skip it." *God, that sounded so fucking pathetic.*

"Deciding you didn't need a birthday lets everyone else off the hook, but it means you don't get a special day." Rowan was matter of fact, but the observation made Gideon feel bereft as if he'd missed out on all those special days over the years.

I still haven't let go of his hand.

Rowan sat back and slipped straight into thoughtful mode, something he did when he had a particularly thorny decision to make at work. Gideon filled the time until Rowan inevitably tried to fix things by breaking off small bits of the pastry marveling at the flaky goodness as he ate it. He actually offered Rowan some but Rowan was still in thinking mode and shook his head.

"It's all yours." There was another moment of silence, and then Rowan let out an enthusiastic aha! "Next June you can send a gift to Kaden."

"I can?"

"Of course. He and Ryan have birthdays close to each other so get them a hotel stay or a spa day or something like that."

"Uh huh. Kaden likes cars, maybe I could do a track day or…something."

"Exactly! Then you can start a new family tradition where you celebrate each other's special days." Rowan was so pleased with himself that Gideon went with the flow and concentrated back on his pastry.

The final bite was mostly icing, and it was sticky sweet and utterly perfect. An enormous flow of peace swamped Gideon when Rowan leaned into him and rested his head on Gideon's shoulder. They stayed that way for a while, and it was as if they were meant to be there, facing the winter ocean on a blustery cold day. Rowan didn't move, but Gideon knew him so well that he understood Rowan was always thinking about something. When they were in the office, it could be as far ranging as poking at details for an upcoming meeting right up to why a certain tie was good for Gideon to wear. That was the best part of Rowan, he never stopped looking for ways to make Bryant & Waites better, or forcing Gideon to smile, or making Gideon feel like he was…

Cared for?

"Gideon?"

"Yeah?"

"Can I ask you something private?" Rowan asked, his gaze fixed on the rolling waves, gusts of wind swirling around them. He was so serious. He wouldn't look at Gideon even though Gideon had shuffled to face him as best he could.

"I don't know why you're wanting permission because you're going to ask me anyway."

Rowan smirked, and that familiar quirk of his lips was so sexy. "You know me so well. So, what would you normally do on your birthday? I mean, we're not at work, but I know you always have your phone on you. Do you work? Do you see your family? Or meet friends? A boyfriend?"

"I wouldn't hold your hand if I had a boyfriend," Gideon mumbled.

"Friends hold hands." Rowan finally shuffled to turn and face Gideon. "Right?"

They stared at each other, a sudden gust of icy air carrying snow whipped around them. It didn't matter about the cold, all that mattered was that somehow the two of them appeared to be having a *moment*.

"Yes."

"Friends can tell each other all kinds of things, like about their family, I mean you've met mine, and you know them all, so you could tell me about yours."

Oh. So this was the *family* talk.

"You know most of it. Grandparents no longer with us, parents divorced, and my sister, Grace, who shared most of the burden." A bit too late, he should never have said that last part. God knows how much Rowan understood about him already, but the last thing Gideon wanted to do was rake over his private life with him. *Maybe Rowan won't comment on it.* He pushed the conversation forward. "Kaden's the only extended family I've ever had anything to do with—"

"Your family is a burden to you?" Rowan interrupted, and Gideon knew it was too good to be true for Rowan to leave this. He was like a dog with a bone when he got his teeth into something.

"What do you want me to say? I'm not sure it's the right thing to be talking to you about family, or my birthday, or—"

"You're my friend, remember? I paid you to be a friend."

"No, you didn't."

"Yes, I did."

"No, you invited me to…never mind." It was easier to give up.

"So, *friend*, tell me more."

"I hate you," Gideon said without heat.

"No, you don't," Rowan quickly countered.

"And you're fired."

"No, I'm not."

Gideon felt protected here, isolated even apart from Rowan sitting next to him, enough that he had an insane urge to explain. Where were his parents today? Would they be thinking back to the day he was born?

"There's not much to tell. Not everyone has a family like yours," he began. "Some of us just have two sets of parents who have their own lives and only see them on Christmas, weddings, and funerals."

Rowan squeezed Gideon's hand. "You can have my family if you like, not to keep obvs."

"Obvs," Gideon repeated.

"You can borrow them for birthdays and weddings, but it does mean you need to visit with me at least four times a year, and also invite them to the city for theater trips and stayovers. How does that sound?"

Rowan was probably teasing him, but the concept of a family for hire sounded weirdly perfect right now. He didn't know them that well, but Rowan's moms were cool. They worried about their children, and took in dogs, and had undeniably welcomed him into their house without comment. "Okay," he murmured, hoping that the word was carried away by the wind, and that he hadn't just committed himself to some weird-ass family for hire nonsense. Rowan leaned away from him, released his hand, and then stood up, brushing snow from his pants and frowning down at the seat as if it had personally decided to make his ass damp.

Rowan looked…windblown, sexy…but now was not the time to give in to admiring his thoughtful, gorgeous, annoying, sexy PA. Gideon stood up, but when he looked at Rowan, he was staring at him, which caused him to pause before putting his gloves back on. They were standing too close, the sound of the ocean and the gusts of cold snowy wind a backdrop to whatever was happening here.

Rowan took a step nearer, and they were as close as they could be without touching.

"Gideon?" Rowan whispered, and that was all he said. He didn't invite Gideon to cup his face or to tug him that final short distance, but that's what Gideon did. He didn't ask to be kissed, but if Gideon stopped now they might never kiss at all. It was the right moment, the perfect time, when they were alone, away from the office and family and friends. It was now or never.

Gideon's hands still cradled Rowan's face, and for a moment, they paused as Gideon looked into Rowan's dark eyes.

"What am I doing?" he said, but Rowan didn't answer. Instead, they met in the middle with a gentle sweet touch of lips before separating.

Gideon's heart beat hard, every exposed inch of skin tingled, and they stared at each other. This was wrong, this was a boss taking advantage, this would ruin everything they had between them, he had to stop it now when they could still laugh this off as nothing. This time there was no alcohol, no post-wedding aura. Was there really a way to excuse them sharing a kiss this time?

"We should—"

Rowan didn't give Gideon a chance to talk. He took the initiative, and it was his turn to begin a kiss. Wrapping his hands around Gideon's neck, he *kissed* him. From a gentle exploration, it soon became more. A desperate need to taste that overtook Gideon in a frenzy. He wanted to feel Rowan against him, wanted to press him to a wall, take his fill of these needy kisses.

Somehow, he managed to move them so that Rowan was cradled between the wall of the shelter and Gideon. The powerful anticipation of taking care of Rowan was nearly too much, but the gusts of snow reminding them they were in public was enough to keep Gideon from having his hands all over Rowan.

Their coats were too bulky for Gideon to really feel Rowan, but if Rowan was half as hard as he was right now...they could get off here. They could grind against each other, and deepen the kiss, and...

Rowan pulled back and away, a finger to his lips, and he looked dazed. "Oh," he muttered, and Gideon winced when he imagined that Rowan's next words would be a denial of what they'd done or a comment about work relationships. "That was..." For a moment, he stood there, and Gideon waited for more. Then in a quick move he had an armful of Rowan, and they were kissing again, a hundred kinds of frantic and needy.

So much for work relationships being ruined—this was all about lust.

The next time they separated Rowan was grinning, but he didn't go back in for more kisses. Instead, he put on his gloves, fixed his coat, and picked up the plastic tub. "We should...yeah...maybe get going."

Gideon took a moment to rearrange himself and caught Rowan staring at him with a hungry gaze. He so nearly dragged Rowan toward him for more kissing. They made it all the way to the van, and even though it wasn't far, it was enough time for Gideon to begin second guessing himself. He glanced at Rowan and wondered if he was having similar thoughts.

"Stop it," Rowan warned and then smiled. "That was inevitable. It's been building since the day you hired me."

"It has?"

Rowan laughed then, and the sound of it made Gideon smile. He added a shimmy, and a turn, and then pointed at himself. "Plus who can resist all of this?"

"I have resisted," Gideon reminded him.

"In your dreams," Rowan replied. "Wedding?"

"I think you instigated then."

"You lingered," Rowan reminded him and unlocked the van.

Inside they sat for a moment, and Rowan reached for his hand. One more time they sat hand in hand, but when Gideon leaned in for another kiss, he was certain that Rowan would want it, and would be there to kiss him back.

He did.

This was turning out to be the best birthday.

"Should we talk about this?" Gideon asked as they neared the house. He was dazed, insecure, unsure, worried, turned on, confused. God, he didn't know what he was.

Rowan parked and killed the engine. "Let's just leave talking for the moment, yeah?"

He kissed Gideon one last time, and they climbed out of the vehicle. Rowan pulled his beanie down over his ears and cursed at the sudden cold while Gideon watched for any sign that Rowan regretted the kiss. There was nothing.

"Let's go into the house quickly," Rowan

announced, not quite meeting Gideon's gaze, and held out a hand to tug him toward the big house, but Gideon wanted a quiet place to talk.

Or kiss.

He was happy with either, but maybe talking would stop the kissing or kissing might mean they never talk and *fuck*, it was a mess.

"I thought maybe we should talk or—"

"After," Rowan interrupted and opened the front door of his moms' place. They took off coats and boots, and then Rowan stood in front of him, fussing with Gideon's hair, then his own, which was a mess of flicks after beanie-use, before straightening his sweater. "Let's go."

He opened the front room door and gestured for Gideon to go in first, which wasn't odd, but for some reason, Gideon was nervous. What was wrong? Why wouldn't Rowan look him in the eyes? Was he regretting what they'd done? Had Gideon completely fucked up everything? He took a step into the room and stumbled back into Rowan at the bright lights, glaring colors, and overwhelming noise.

"Surprise!"

ELEVEN

Rowan

———————

"Go on. Put it on." Rowan sucked the icing from his thumb and side-eyed Gideon. The two of them were sitting together on one of the sofas. Gideon at one end, or close to because Deon had crammed himself in the space between Gideon and the arm of the couch. Deon had his butt in the air, and his face and front paws on Gideon's thigh and looked to be settled for the night. Rowan ended up in the middle, with Ava curled up at the other side of him currently absorbed in a text conversation. Rowan figured it was with her ex.

Does he want her back? Or is she chasing after him?

Mom, Momo, and Kevin's wife, Esther, were in the kitchen. Kevin himself was down on the floor with his older daughter and Sarah's kids, while Sarah and her husband were upstairs, dropping off their bags, having just arrived ten minutes ago.

"You need to wear the hat." Clara, Kevin's youngest, announced and pointed at Gideon.

Gideon raised his hands. He looked uncomfortable despite the smile he wore. "I'm all right. But thank you." His tone was soft.

So, he does know how to talk to children.

Gideon chuckled but it sounded off somehow, forced, awkward.

Or maybe not.

"Uncle Rowan." Clara glared at him as if it was his fault Gideon wasn't playing along.

"Yes, yes." Rowan wiped his hands together then took the party hat from her hand. "Now, now, Mr. Gideon, you must wear your hat. It's a party after all." He held the cone hat in one hand and gently tugged on the thin elastic. He met Gideon's gaze and wiggled his finger for Gideon to lean forward.

"But…" Though he protested, Gideon leaned over.

Rowan positioned the hat and straightened the elastic that would hold it in place. "A birthday boy needs a hat."

"And where's your hat?" Gideon asked and sat back. He gently touched his hair where Rowan's fingers had brushed. There was a gentle smile at the corner of his mouth.

What is this feeling? They hadn't had a chance to talk about their kiss from earlier or about crossing the line they had stood on either side of for all these years. The line between a boss and his PA.

We need to talk about it.

"My hat?" Rowan arched his neck. "I think I took it off when I was checking out the snacks." He smiled and poked Clara in the small of her back, her attention had turned to the brightly colored children's show on the television. The sound was muted, but the cartoon characters seemed to move in a way that matched the music Momo had set playing on the stereo.

Clara looked up at him. Her big blue eyes were the same as her mother's. Although Rowan had found the shape of her nose and mouth reminded him of Kevin.

"Can you go get my hat for me? It's on the table." He pointed across the room.

Clara simply nodded and scurried away. Rowan tilted his head and couldn't help but smile.

"You're better with children than I imagined," Gideon mused.

"Really?"

Gideon stared at where Kevin was playing with the others. "You're always so organized, like things just so. Children equal chaos and are unpredictable. I thought you'd find them difficult."

Rowan quirked an eyebrow. He guessed he'd never really talked to Gideon about his family or his nieces and nephews. There'd always been this wall around Gideon when family was mentioned, he'd always seem uncomfortable, distracted as if backing away from those types of conversations.

I guess I have a small idea why since the talk at the ocean.

"You mean I should be cooing about them more when we're back at the office?" Gideon's nose crinkled as he eyed Kevin and the children. "I think you'd have a harder time handling them than me with your fancy office, furniture, suits, the way you alphabetize your vinyl collection."

"I don't—" Gideon interjected.

Rowan slid sideways, resting against Gideon's shoulder. Gideon tensed for a moment then relaxed. Rowan smiled, purposely brushed the side of his hand against Gideon's leg. "Actually, in some ways you're not wrong. I mean kids are messy, noisy, ridiculous at times. But it's different when they're family, isn't it? I love them." He leaned in closer. "Plus, Uncle Rowan can wind them up, fill them with sugar, then hand them back at the end of the day. Win-win."

Gideon nodded. "I see." He moved his fingers, gently sliding them between Rowan's.

Warm.

"Uncle Rowan." Clara was running back toward them. The card hat dangling at her side as she clutched the elastic.

"Whoa," he said, scooping her up before she bumped into Gideon's leg. "Remember Gideon hurt his knee."

Clara arched her neck, her head ending up in Gideon's lap right next to Deon's head as she squirmed. "Because of Bear?"

"That's right." Rowan held his hand above her face like a claw, wiggling his fingers. "So be careful." He tickled her neck, and she squealed and wriggled in his arms.

Deon lifted his head, howled along with Clara's lively sounds, and Clara sunk lower into the space between Rowan's knees and kicked out her tiny foot catching Ava's arm.

Ava yelped.

"Oops." Rowan grabbed hold of Clara's feet and turned to find Ava looking pissed. "Sorry."

With a sigh, Ava picked up her phone from where it had been knocked from her hands and had fallen into her lap. She glanced at the screen, and then at Clara, before putting her cell on the arm of the couch with an expression that said she was done with whoever she'd been talking to. "I want in on some tickle action too." She knocked her shoulder to Rowan's as she went for Clara's stomach.

Clara let out a high-pitched scream, and Rowan winced.

So loud.

She flipped over, half-laughing, half-grumbling as she slid to her knees on the floor. Deon jumped down with her, his tail wagging so hard it was causing a breeze. She caught her breath, tugged her skirt down over her woolen tights, and got up onto unsteady feet. "Daddy." Clara ran at Kevin, jumping up his back and circling her arms around his neck. She glanced back at them.

Deon followed behind, sniffing at Dog who was curled up at Kevin's side, before sitting down beside her.

"You know Clara'll be back wanting you to do it again before long," Rowan said.

Ava tutted. "I know."

"Row, row, row your boat…" Rowan teased.

"Ugh, shut it. My arms ache thinking about it."

"Huh?" Gideon said.

Rowan chuckled. "She was playing with Clara this one time. Was it last year? Anyway, whenever it was, they were *rowing* their boat. Clara was on Ava's knees and Ava pulled her back and forth and back and forth." He motioned his hand. "And well, I can't even remember how long they were at it."

Ava punched his arm. "And you just sat there laughing."

"I'd already learned my lesson with Phoebe. Do you know how many times in a row I watched *Frozen*?" He met her eyes. "Four. Four times."

She pressed her lips together, failed to suppress her smirk. "Let it—"

He clamped his hand over her mouth. "Don't you dare."

She mumbled into his palm though it sounded as if she was just making noise rather than particular words. Her cheeks plumped as something warm and wet pushed against his hand.

"Eww," Rowan said and pulled his hand back. "You actually licked me." He flapped his hand around and then wiped it on the shoulder of her hoodie. "Gross."

Ava stuck out her tongue then picked up her phone. The family interlude was over, and she was back to frowning.

Rowan sighed. "Anyway." He bent over, picked up the paper hat Clara had left on the floor, then leaned into Gideon, and looked up to meet his gaze. His eyes were bright, though his brow was creased, an expression he had worn several times over the last couple of days. It was as if Rowan and his messy, extended family confused him.

"How is your knee?" Rowan asked. He turned the hat in his hand before putting it on, positioning it at an angle to one side.

Gideon gently rubbed above his knee. "The bruises are still there. Obvs." He chuckled. "But the swelling has gone down so I'm sure it'll be fine now."

"That's good." He rested his head on Gideon's shoulder and patted Gideon's chest.

"Tired?"

"A bit. My family wears me out." He turned his face slightly so that his lips were pressed to the top of Gideon's arm above the material of his sweater.

"But you like it, don't you?" Gideon placed his hand over Rowan's.

Rowan blinked, cast his gaze over his home and the people in it. "Yep."

I wouldn't change it for the world.

"Give me a hand for a minute."

Rowan raised an eyebrow, Kevin was standing over him, looking serious. "What with?"

"In the kitchen."

"Really?"

Kevin rolled his eyes, grabbed Rowan by the wrist, and tugged on his arm. "Just come help me."

"Okay, okay." He let Kevin help him off the couch. "You need anything while I'm up?" he asked Gideon.

"Not right now." Gideon held a half-full glass of beer in his hand.

Rowan followed Kevin through to the kitchen. It was just the two of them. "So, what do you need me for?"

Kevin put his hands on his hips and with a straight face asked, "Are you drunk?"

"Am I...?" Rowan scratched the back of his neck. He'd had a couple of beers, a glass of wine he'd managed to steal from the bottle Ava had been nursing all night. He might be relaxed, happy, but definitely not drunk. "No. Ava on the other hand..." He met Kevin's eyes.

Why does he look so serious?

"Did I do something?" Rowan tapped his chin, trying to think of what had happened over the last few hours. The birthday celebration had turned into the more common Christmas Eve family fun and games. "Pretty sure I didn't declare Santa a fake this year."

Kevin's eyes widened. "*This* year? The kids, you didn't—"

Rowan gripped Kevin's shoulder before he spiraled into fatherly despair. "Joke. It's a joke." He shrugged. "If it's about my performance during charades. I just suck at it, drunk or not."

With a sigh, Kevin shook his head. "Can we be serious for a moment?"

"Okay." Rowan leaned back against the kitchen counter. Laughter echoed through from the other room.

Was Gideon okay in there? The children would be heading to bed shortly, leaving the adults to prepare for tomorrow.

"Is it okay that you're…" Kevin waved his hand in front of him.

Rowan tilted his head. "I'm what?"

"…getting all touchy-feely with him? Is that okay? He's your boss, isn't he?"

With Gideon? Ah. I was? Rowan chewed on his thumbnail.

"Have you no self-awareness?"

"Well, are you saying I shouldn't get touchy-feely with him?" His heart clenched at the thought of Kevin or anybody telling him otherwise. The reaction surprised him.

"That's not what I'm saying, or why I'm saying anything." Kevin stepped closer. "I just wanted to make sure you were okay."

"Why wouldn't I be?"

"You like to please people. I think we both know that, and well…"

Rowan stared Kevin's feet. "Ah, the stockings," he said.

"Please don't say it out loud again." Kevin shook his head.

"We were kids," he tried to dismiss the incident. He thought back to when Kevin had found him that time. It was before he had come out to the rest of the family. Back then, Kevin's only concern had been him, had *he* been okay. Maybe it had shown on his face he hadn't been, despite having agreed to go along with the other boy's fetish.

That boy had asked, so I did it, I wore the stockings and let him bind my hands with his school tie. I'd wanted him to like me. I didn't want to be thrown away.

When Rowan raised his head, Kevin was looking at him. His expression radiated his usual gentle strength.

Kevin smiled. "Hey. What's with the face?"

Rowan touched his cheek, wondering what kind of face he was pulling. "I don't know."

"If it's something you've decided on your own then there's not a problem and I say go for it." Kevin smiled. "I just felt I needed to ask for my own peace of mind. I know the others will say I'm being too nosy, and you're not exactly my *little* brother anymore, but…"

"Thanks," Rowan said. "Yes, Gideon's my boss, but whatever happens, it'll be because I want it to. He would never take advantage. He's not like that."

Kevin nodded. "I guess I worried over nothing. If it's what you want, I'm glad." He snorted a soft laugh. "You've changed a little, you know?"

"I have?"

"Yeah, I think so. Seems you're able to do things for yourself now, not just for those around you." He pressed his lips together. "I'm only realizing it now, but I think maybe you changed a while ago." He squeezed Rowan's shoulder. "It suits you." He took a deep breath. "Right, I need to go and help wrangle the kids to bed."

"Sure."

Kevin left the kitchen.

I've changed? Had he really? Wanting to change had been the reason he had taken the job at Bryant & Waites in the first place. He smiled to himself. Just as Kevin hadn't realized, maybe he hadn't himself. He actually *had* been moving forward all this time.

"Man, it's so cold," Rowan said in a hushed voice and stomped his feet on the snowy ground. He glanced back at the house aware of the people already asleep. Kevin and his family had headed for their cabin a few hours ago, while Sarah's two were in one of the rooms upstairs.

"Three minutes," Gideon said and slipped his cell phone into his coat.

"To what?"

"Christmas."

"Ugh, seriously? When did it get so late? Sorry about that." Rowan stretched his neck from side to side.

Gideon bumped his elbow to Rowan's. "I had fun."

"You sure? Probably not how you imagined celebrating your birthday this year."

Gideon chuckled. "Actually, it was better."

"Really?"

"Really. I haven't had a *good* birthday in a very long time. Not really."

Rowan linked his arm in Gideon's. He wanted to hear more, but he also didn't. It was enough to know Gideon had enjoyed himself amidst the chaos called Rowan's family. They walked in a comfortable silence back to the cabin, and he shelved the questions he had for a later time.

"Gideon," Rowan said when they stepped inside.

"Yeah?" Gideon closed the door and turned to face Rowan. "What—" His words were cut off as Rowan grabbed his face and pulled him into a long kiss.

Ah, warm.

Rowan moved his mouth, gently brushing Gideon's lips with his tongue. He breathed in through his nose and eventually parted. "I've been wanting to do that all night."

What I want. He thought back to his conversation with Kevin.

"Yeah?"

"How about you?" He grinned at Gideon's surprised expression. "I know we've not had a chance to talk about it properly, so if you regret earlier, we can chalk it up to this being nothing more than a Christmas kiss. We can say I was filled with Christmas spirit—"

Gideon clamped his hand over Rowan's mouth. "Stop talking." He lowered his hand, leaving Rowan expectant, and he wasn't disappointed when Gideon grabbed the front of his coat, pulled him close, and kissed him firmly.

They stood together, Gideon's back to the door, one hand holding Rowan in place, the other lifting the bottom of Rowan's jacket, seeking entry beneath the numerous layers to squeeze the flesh of his hip.

They kissed for a long time. Rowan pressed one hand to Gideon's chest and with his other, he threaded his fingers through the back of Gideon's hair.

This is what I want.

The kiss went on, heat flushing his body.

Too hot. Too many layers.

"Say, Gideon?" he said when they finally parted.

"What?" Gideon asked, catching his breath. His eyes were glazed, and he almost looked as desperate as Rowan felt for the two of them to connect.

Rowan hugged his neck, pressed his mouth to Gideon's ear, and whispered, "How's the knee?"

TWELVE

Gideon

"The knee's good," Gideon lied and slipped his hand under Rowan's sweater and the T-shirt underneath to find skin. Rowan hissed at the touch, and Gideon immediately moved his hand, only for Rowan to grip it hard and put it back in the exact same place.

"Cold hands but more," Rowan demanded and wrapped his hands around Gideon's neck, and a rush of desire consumed Gideon. He'd spent so long looking at Rowan, wondering about him and stopping himself from going anywhere *near* Rowan, and now they were here, and it blew his mind. With exaggerated care he unwrapped Rowan's hands from his neck and stepped back a little so there was space between them. They stared at each other in a weirdly erotic face-off. Rowan's tongue darted out to taste their kisses, his lips shiny. He very deliberately moved his hands down his body then unzipped his jeans at the same time as toeing off his boots. With the denim loose, the length of his hard cock was visible under the material of his jersey shorts, and Gideon couldn't take his eyes off what was on offer.

"I'm not making you do this," he blurted.

"No," Rowan murmured. "You're not." He slipped a hand under the band and pushed the denim and jersey down so that it rested on his thighs. His T-shirt shifted and covered the prize, but he slipped the jacket off his shoulders and then pulled the T-shirt up and over his head. That was Gideon's first look at his efficient PA unwrapped and standing *right there*. "You're wearing too many clothes."

Gideon took another step back, his left calf meeting one of the single beds. This moment was pivotal. It wasn't just sex, but it might be destroying his working relationship with Rowan.

"What about when we get back?"

Rowan shrugged and circled his cock with his hand, giving it a couple of gentle tugs, and bit his lip. Fuck, it was like Rowan was giving his own personal porn show. Gideon had never seen anything so beautiful as Rowan leaning back against the wall, slipping his hands around his cock, and every so often running his thumb over the head then thrusting into curled fingers, and all the goddamn time he was nibbling on his lip.

Jesus.

"We should talk," Gideon said, when, in reality, the last thing he wanted to do was talk at all. As far as he could see he had two options, step forward toward Rowan or call an end to this.

Rowan slid a hand up his body, touching a cinnamon nipple on his dark hair covered chest, pulling it and gently twisting it. The noise he let out, a soft sigh, and the way his other hand was moving on his cock sent sparks of fire through every one of Gideon's nerves. He was so hard that he either locked himself in the bathroom or accepted the invitation in Rowan's hooded gaze.

It was all *too much*.

"I want you," Gideon said. "Just to make things clear, so we're not...doing..."

"I want you," Rowan agreed and twisted his hand on his cock again.

"What if it's wrong?"

Rowan tilted his head in thought. "What if it isn't?"

Gideon was burning up, the temptation right in front of him, Rowan waiting for him to do anything, and he wanted to move. *I have to move.*

"You're so sexy." As soon as the words left Gideon's mouth, he moved, two strides, and he had an armful of Rowan. In a smooth move, he shoved the denim and jersey lower and helped Rowan until he was completely naked. Gideon was on his knees, which hurt like a bitch, but he wasn't going to lose this moment. "Can I?" he asked for permission, his hands flat on Rowan's thighs. Rowan's cock right there within reach.

"How about we take this to the bed, and you get out of your clothes?" Rowan sounded concerned, and the last thing that Gideon wanted was Rowan to fret over the knee, or the floor, or the heat in the room, or the light, or any freaking thing.

"Nuh-uh," Gideon managed, tracing his hands to Rowan's ass, gripping and tugging him forward. He pressed kisses to Rowan's thigh then to the other moving his way closer to the intended target. His first taste of Rowan was heaven. The weight of his cock on Gideon's tongue was the most erotic thing he'd ever felt. He teased the head with his lips and tongue, nibbling his way around and then swallowing the tip until his lips met Rowan's hand. He spent the longest time kneading Rowan's ass and sucking on the tip of his cock until the moment Rowan moved his hand, and then it was game on.

He put his own hand on Rowan's cock and abruptly lost the ability to stand upright.

"Bed…" Rowan pleaded, and Gideon was up for that as long as he got more time to suck and lick every inch of his beauty. He released his hold on Rowan and gave his new lover's cock one last suck before scrambling to stand, wincing at his knee but ignoring it. Shoving at his clothes, pulling, throwing, not caring where any of it landed until he could join Rowan on the bed, stopping halfway and heading for the one thing he wanted right now. Rowan's cock in his mouth. Gideon sucked him down. Rowan groaned. And only when Rowan gripped his hair and tugged him up did he move, sliding up Rowan's body to half cover him and then easing between his spread legs.

Finally, stiff cock met stiff cock, and they kissed with desperation, sliding and rutting against each other.

"This is dangerous," he whispered as he kissed Rowan's heated skin concentrating on his neck. Leaving a trail of kisses up to his lips, he pulled Rowan closer so they could deepen the kiss.

His balls were tight. He was overwhelmed. He'd never felt anything like this, and it didn't matter if it was right for the company, it was right for them at this moment. One taste of Rowan and he was addicted.

"You got any protection?" Rowan asked, and Gideon whimpered into his throat. Condoms were the very last thing he'd thought of bringing with him on a Christmas family visit. He'd packed gift cards, and his shaving kit, a couple of suits, and that was it.

"None. Shit."

"Okay, then we do it this way for now, but when we can, I want you to fuck me. You get that?" Rowan was fierce, and Gideon looked into stunning brown eyes and saw the promise in them. "I want you to show me everything you feel for me, fuck me over my desk, in the file room, in your place, mine. I want to steal kisses and hold your head as I fuck your mouth."

"Stop." How was it that someone as sassy but innocent seeming as Rowan knew how to talk with sex dripping from every syllable?

"No, I won't. I've wanted you so long, dreamed of you forcing me up against the filing cabinet, tearing off my pants and falling to your knees and sucking me until I'm dry then turning me around. There'd be so much lube, and you'd press inside me, and I would grip that cabinet as you fucked me into next week."

"Rowan—"

Gideon was so close. He wanted all that, every second of it. Wanted to push Rowan to his knees, over his desk, anywhere that was safe where he could show

Rowan what he felt. Orgasm chased down his spine, but he wanted Rowan to go over the edge first.

"My turn," he said thickly and pinned Rowan's hands above his head. "I'll do that. I'll open you up for me, put my fingers in you. How many can you take? One? I'll push it in. I'll find your sweet spot, and I will make you fucking come without touching yourself. I won't let you move. You like that?"

Rowan closed his eyes and gasped. His neck was exposed for bites, and then he arched and cursed, "*Fuck!*" It was hot and wet between them.

He went limp in Gideon's grasp, but Gideon wasn't gentle, slipping and sliding in Rowan's cum on his skin. He found a rhythm, and in a few thrusts Gideon came so hard he closed his eyes and cursed and buried his face in Rowan's neck.

They lay tangled, hot, and sticky until their breathing returned to normal.

"You have a filthy mouth," Gideon muttered, pressing lazy kisses on the skin he could reach, desperate to never move again.

"Says the man who wants to finger me in the file room," Rowan said and moved his head so they could kiss properly.

"I will never be able to go into that file room again and not think about doing that," Gideon admitted.

"I'll be there waiting for you." Rowan smiled into the kiss.

That sounded suspiciously as if he was describing a future. As if Rowan wanted this to carry on past tonight. *Is that what I want?*

A cool breeze slid over their skin, and Gideon couldn't help shivering. Part of him wanted to pull the covers over them and not to move at all, but that would be the most wrong thing he'd ever done. Instead, he reluctantly disengaged from Rowan's grip then held out a hand and made a small step into a nebulous future.

"Shower?"

They padded into the bathroom. Gideon started the water before Rowan pulled him into an embrace and kissed him hard. If he didn't stop that Gideon couldn't be held responsible for what happened next. Sex. More kissing. More sex. That was what was going to happen next if Rowan didn't stop because Gideon was getting hard again. It might just be his cock making a valiant try, but the thought of Rowan up against that damn cabinet, writhing on Gideon's fingers in his ass…

They washed off in silence, there was more kissing than washing, and when Rowan went to his knees, water sliding over his shoulders, Gideon's cock was very interested in a second round. So much for losing the will the moment he got past thirty. Rowan sucked him down, played with his balls, bit and kissed and sucked every inch, and this time when he was coming, splashing his spend on Rowan's neck as the water sluiced it away, he couldn't help the yelp. When he watched Rowan getting himself off, soaping his hands, sliding along his cock before coming with a shout, Gideon knew this was a long way past dangerous.

This was an addiction, for real.

They didn't wear anything to bed, opting to share one bed, curled up against each other. Gideon the little spoon with Rowan's heat against his back, the covers tucked up around them.

"Breakfast is at seven," he whispered and Gideon heard beeps as Rowan set an alarm on his watch.

"It will be chaos, won't it?" Gideon said.

"It will, so if you want to stay here, I'll come back later on in the day."

"No, I want to go. I have gifts to give."

"You do? You didn't have to do that, but it is so thoughtful and very sweet."

Gideon's heart warmed at the soft praise and comfortably wrapped in Rowan's arms, he slept.

Christmas Day was mayhem and madness layered over chaos and noise. It was bright-colored paper and squealing kids and hugs and kisses. Gideon and Rowan shared one chair, out of necessity. Gideon sat on the cushion, and Rowan was perched on the edge. After a while, Gideon tugged Rowan down so that he was half-sitting on his lap and only when Rowan was in his arms did Gideon feel at peace.

There were some gifts for Gideon. A beard grooming kit from the moms, specialty shampoos from Rowan's sister, and other smelly stuff.

Rowan gifted him a mug with the words "Best Boss" on it and a beautiful silk tie in a shade of blue watercolor pattern.

"This will make my eyes pop," he said to Rowan

then reached up and tugged him down for a kiss. "You said so."

Rowan smiled into the kiss and pulled back a little.

"That's why I got it for you," Rowan said. "I love…" He stopped, and a million tiny messages telegraphed in his eyes. "…the way your beautiful eyes change color when you wear blue."

"Have you been looking at my eyes?"

"Since the day I started working at Bryant & Waites."

"What about the rest?" It seemed as if the noise of Christmas faded away as Rowan stared down at him.

Rowan's gaze was guarded. "The rest?"

Gideon was doing this wrong. He had so much to say, but it wasn't fair for Rowan to have to answer first. It was his turn to strip himself bare the way Rowan had done last night but using his words and pure honesty.

"I've been looking at you since the moment I offered you a bottle of water in the interview," he admitted cautiously and waited for Rowan to laugh at him.

Rowan smiled so beautifully then pressed one final kiss to Gideon's lips. "Same here."

"Break it up!" Kevin said and tossed a stuffed teddy bear at them, which hit Rowan square on the head and led to Rowan and Kevin rolling about on the floor like idiots. When the kids joined in, Gideon slipped out to the kitchen to find another can of soda.

"Escaping the chaos?" Jodie asked from where she was refilling a jug of some cocktail that she and Gill apparently drank on Christmas Day. It was a tradition going back to the first day they met. If he and Rowan did that, then they'd be drinking water every time they wanted to recognize the day they met.

The thought made him smile.

"Yeah, Christmas is normally me, a film, and avoiding family."

She carefully placed the jug on the table and pressed a hand to Gideon's chest.

"Be kind to him," she said with a soft warning tone. "Don't shut him out and remember who he is."

Of course, Gideon would remember who he was, but he had to reassure Jodie. He captured her hand and squeezed it. "I will."

THIRTEEN

Rowan

"I ate too much," Rowan whined and rested his head on Gideon's chest. He flinched when Gideon rubbed his side. This was the first moment Deon had left Gideon's side, and Rowan was taking advantage of the extra space.

"You certainly did." Gideon pinched him through his sweater.

"Gids, if you don't want to see dinner again, I suggest you stop that."

Gideon rested his palm over Rowan's stomach.

The two of them were lying together on one couch. The day had passed in a whirl of presents, family, and food, and Rowan was exhausted.

"So, how was it?" He idly drew his finger in circles over Gideon's sweater, teasing one of his shirt buttons that lay beneath. "Christmas with this bunch of weirdos?"

Gideon caught Rowan's hand and raised it to press a kiss to his palm. "Perfectly chaotic."

Rowan laughed, curled his hand so he brushed Gideon's jaw. "Is that a good thing?"

"Definitely." He leaned into Rowan's touch. "It's different from what I'm used to, but I didn't hate it. Also, it was nice to get to see into your world. You tend to stop talking when your family comes up."

Rowan stroked Gideon's hand. *So he had noticed.*

"My world, huh? Even though it's messy and complicated? Oh, and loud. So very loud." He sighed and closed his eyes. Gideon's body was warm and his heartbeat steady. Rowan was so very comfortable and would be happy to fall asleep right there beside Gideon.

As if I didn't have a care in the world.

"Aren't most families?"

Rowan opened his eyes and arched his neck to look up at Gideon.

Gideon said, "Though I think you take loud to a whole other level."

Rowan pursed his lips and stared at the other sofa where Ava was laying on her stomach. A variety of Christmas decorations were draped over her back and pinned to her cardigan as a way of a goodnight present from the children in the family, though the plan was very much instigated by Kevin, the biggest child of them all.

He smiled to himself. It had been an hour since Sarah and her family had headed back to town and home for a more intimate, adult Christmas once the twins were tucked up in bed, and Ava hadn't stirred once since then.

Alcohol and heartbreak. Poor thing.

"We're heading to bed," Kevin said in a hushed voice. Phoebe, the eldest of his daughters, was bundled up in his arms. She was sleeping soundly, her arms limply hanging down, her cheek squashed to Kevin's chest as he hugged her against him all wrapped up in her warm winter coat.

"What a lightweight," Rowan teased and gently rubbed her ankle.

"Night night, Uncle Ro." Kevin put on a childish voice and waved Phoebe's hand. "See you in the morning."

"Behave," Esther chided as she joined him, carrying Clara. Clara was lying on her back with her arms and legs spread wide like a starfish in her orange plump looking jacket. Her mouth was slightly open as she arched her back. Esther sighed, reaffirming her hold. "See you tomorrow," she mouthed and followed after Kevin.

Rowan reached for his cell phone on the sofa cushion. Opening it up, he selected the front camera then raised the phone above them. "Smile," he said.

Gideon leaned in closer as Rowan snapped a shot.

"Another," Rowan said and curled his hand in the front of Gideon's shirt. He tilted his head to pose and was surprised when Gideon pressed a kiss to his forehead. He pressed the screen, the moment captured. "I look terrible," he uttered.

"You look fine." Gideon rested his chin on the top of Rowan's head. "But since it's Christmas, just this once, I'll let you take another."

With a smile, Rowan leaned back his head, managing to catch Gideon's mouth with his for a series of brief kisses. "It's okay. Got the real thing right here." He closed his eyes when Gideon touched under his chin, tilted his face for a firmer, longer kiss.

"Still hungry?" Momo's voice dispelled the magic of the moment. "Plenty of leftovers instead of eating each other's faces." She chuckled from the doorway.

"Leave them alone." Mom playfully whipped Momo's ass with the kitchen towel. With a sigh, she folded the towel and put it on the side, then entered the front room, squeezing Momo's butt as she passed. "And with that, I'm done. Dishes washed, dried, and put away." She glanced at Rowan. "And before you say anything, we don't need one."

Gideon poked Rowan's arm. "Need what?"

Momo chimed in, "A dishwasher." She walked up to where Ava was laying. "That girl could always sleep through anything."

"Let me guess. Kevin?" Mom took a length of tinsel from Ava's back.

"He had help," Rowan said.

"I bet." Mom crouched down beside Ava and gently stroked her hair as Momo removed the rest of the decorations. "Hey." She tickled Ava's neck, eliciting a moan. "Come on. You can't stay here all night."

"Shurrup," Ava muttered and waved her arm in the air.

Momo wore a grin as she dangled tinsel in front of Ava's face, dragging it across her nose.

Ava made a strange sound, some sneeze and splutter

combo, as she rolled onto her back. "I hate you both," she complained, though her words held no weight or intent. She groaned and rubbed at her face. "What time is it?"

"Coming up on ten o'clock."

"Ugh." Ava rested her arm over her face.

Mom stood. "Come on. Let's get you upstairs."

It took both Mom and Momo to get Ava to her feet and upstairs.

"Night," Rowan called after them, chuckling as Ava raised her arm and showed him her middle finger. "Love you too." He gripped Gideon's hand. "Shall we head back too?"

"If you're sure. Did you want some time alone with your moms? I can go back myself if you'd prefer?"

Rowan shook his head. "I think they've earned some time for themselves." With a groan, he leaned forward. "I swear every year I say I've learned my lesson, and yet, same thing, way too much food." He stood up and stretched his arms above his head. "Pretty sure I say something similar every time I get drunk as well." He faced Gideon. "I'm never drinking again." He animated the line with jazz hands then bit his lip, remembering back to Darcy's wedding.

The wedding, that kiss seems so long ago. Wanting to kiss Gideon, but also not wanting to unbalance their relationship, ruin the place and person he'd come to rely on, the person he wanted to be comfortable around, enjoy himself with. He'd tormented himself over the moment. *Things could have gone differently.*

Gideon pushed against the couch and got to his feet. He rested his hand on Rowan's hip. "Are you okay?"

Rowan nodded. "Just taking a moment. Overthinking. You know how it is?" He gripped Gideon's hand. He suddenly felt needy. Rowan wanted to stay close to Gideon and not let go of his hand for fear this thing they had easily settled into would upend itself.

I don't want to screw this up.

"You don't have to leave, you know?" Mom said as she reached the bottom of the stairs.

Rowan met her in a hug. "It's fine. I'm exhausted. Plus I think you and Momo have earned some quiet, just-the-two-of-you time."

"The two of us? I wish. Momo has plans with a certain gentleman this evening." She grinned when Rowan raised an eyebrow in curiosity. "Rod Stewart."

"Again?"

"It's tradition. It's adorable how she's watched it so many times she'll be humming the next song before a single note is played." She smiled fondly.

Rowan pressed a kiss to Mom's cheek. "Well, enjoy the two of you."

"We will."

They collected their coats and headed to the door.

"See you at breakfast," Mom said as she saw them outside.

Rowan blew out a big breath. "Please, no more talk about food." He kissed her again. "Say night to Momo for me."

"Sure." She glanced at Gideon. "Don't let this one eat too much chocolate tomorrow morning."

"Okay," Gideon said.

She patted Rowan's arm. "Chocolate is not breakfast."

"Says who?" Rowan tucked his scarf down the neck of his coat.

"Says me."

Rowan sighed. "Fine. Come on, Gideon."

"I'll keep an eye on him," Gideon said.

"Thanks." Mom hugged herself. "Goodnight." She didn't linger, closing the door to escape the cold.

Rowan stepped down onto the crisp, white ground then stood for a moment. There was a faint flurry of snow in the air, glistening in the outdoor lights. He felt more clearheaded in the fresh air and closed his eyes as he drew a long breath.

"Quiet," he uttered. Though he loved time with his family, he also enjoyed time alone. Calm, peaceful, resting. He opened his eyes when Gideon held his hand and gently pulled for him to follow.

I'm not alone.

This was different from the company of family. Rowan gripped Gideon's hand as they walked. They shared no words but being together was comfortable. This was a different quiet than being alone. He bowed his head, pulled his scarf higher, hiding the smile that had spread across his face. Why did he feel so happy?

They made their way down to the cabin, slipping inside and out of their thick coats.

"Come here," Gideon said and held out his arms.

Having already kicked off his shoes and slipped off his pants and sweater, he had settled on the bed.

Rowan knelt on the bottom of the mattress, trailed his gaze up from Gideon's socks, up his bare legs to the front of his underwear beneath the hem of his shirt.

He looks good.

Gideon patted the space beside him.

Rowan crawled forward. He let out an embarrassing yelp when Gideon wrapped his arms around him and pulled him into a hug. He pressed his hand to his mouth and could feel the heat in his cheeks. What a strange sound he had made.

"Cute," Gideon whispered in his ear and Rowan was convinced his face was beet-red. "I love this." Gideon held him tightly, burying his face in Rowan's hair.

Rowan closed his eyes and hugged Gideon's arm to him. Love. Though Gideon hadn't been exactly talking about him, the word elicited a warmth, which spread through his body.

When was the last time someone told me they loved me? Love in *that* way, romantic, not just his family.

Gideon snuggled close, wriggling to lay properly on the bed.

So warm. So comfortable.

"Your shirt will get creased," Rowan said.

"It's fine." Gideon pressed a kiss to the top of Rowan's head. "I want to stay like this for a while longer."

Rowan leaned his head back, catching Gideon's mouth in a kiss. He smiled. "Me too." He rolled onto his side, draped his leg over Gideon's, and hugged his waist.

"Merry Christmas," he said and settled his head on Gideon's shoulder.

Gideon stroked his hair and pressed more kisses to his hair, forehead, and the end of his nose.

"Love…" Rowan mumbled, sleepily. "…this…too."

FOURTEEN

Gideon
_____

Gideon had mixed feelings about leaving the house and Rowan's family. They were hugging him and making him promise to visit again. He was swept up in the agreement that he would. Not to mention Deon stared miserably at him. If that was even a thing dogs could do.

"I'll miss you, yes I will, yes I will," he dispensed belly rubs and affection to Deon, Dog, and Widget, and even Bear ambled over for some action. Gideon thought he could see guilt in Bear's wide brown eyes. He pressed a kiss to the end of his nose and whispered he forgave him. For a cat-guy, he was certainly being won over by the motley pack of rescues.

As soon as they turned off the property and onto the main road home, he and Rowan were alone. All too soon they would have to face up to what they'd done when they were here, and Gideon quietly worked his way through the concerns until he'd convinced himself of one thing.

Maybe they shouldn't have done what they'd done.

Call it Christmas sparkles, or alcohol, or forced proximity in a snowy cabin, but what happened should have never happened for so many rational reasons. For one, he was Rowan's boss. Away from the influences of the season, he and Rowan had to maintain a corporate relationship that didn't involve Gideon bending his PA over a desk or holding him up against a damn filing cabinet. Also, how was Rowan ever going to respect him as a boss or follow rules or—

"Earth to Gideon, calling Gideon."

Gideon snapped back to reality and glanced at Rowan, who was competently navigating the backroads that would eventually lead to the highway.

"Huh?" he managed when all the breath left his chest and images of making love to this man were so strong in his thoughts. Coherency was the last thing on his list of abilities right now.

"Your thought bubbles are getting in my way," he grouched and made a show of shoving at an imaginary bubble while driving with one hand.

"Hands on the wheel," Gideon warned.

Rowan rolled his eyes and gave the thought bubble one last shove, wincing and pretending it snapped back and hit him. "Seriously, open a window and let them out."

"You're an idiot."

"You're overthinking."

Gideon huffed. "You're my PA."

"You're overthinking."

"You work for me."

"You. Are. Overthinking," Rowan said with an exaggerated sigh.

Gideon subsided into silence. Arms crossed over his chest, watching the countryside pass them by. Freaking Rowan and his stupid ass thought bubbles were going to be the death of him, and now they'd gone a step further and actually got each other off. They'd crossed that line between boss and employee. That wasn't going to end well.

"I promise I won't ask you to fuck me over the desk when we have clients in the office," Rowan stated. "Does that help?"

"What the hell?"

"I know what you're thinking." He put on the annoying fake voice that Gideon hated, the one he used whenever he was schooling Gideon in how to act in polite company. "Hell, we got each other off. Oh no, I want to fuck Rowan over my desk. Oh shit, what if a client sees that, and jeez, what if Rowan doesn't respect me anymore? Not to mention I really like Rowan, and we're friends, and oh shit, have I fucked it all up?"

Gideon side-eyed him then faced front. So what if Rowan was mostly right about all that? Not about the client thing, after all the office door had a lock and the windows had blinds, but still, the respect they had achieved working together.

"I am not thinking any of that," he lied.

"Yes, you are," Rowan insister. He pulled off the road in front of a gate to a wide-open field then killed the engine. "And I am too."

For the first time in a long while Gideon was at a loss for words. "You are?"

"Of course I am. I love my job. If you said I was fired, and that I wouldn't able to do it anymore, I'd be gutted. Not only do I love the people and making sense of the chaos and what we do, but I love working for your grumpy ass the most."

"I wouldn't tell you that you were fired," Gideon defended. "I have no grounds to fire you."

"You're missing the point, Gids," he grumbled and placed his hands on the steering wheel, resting his head on them momentarily.

"What point?"

"The one where I tell you how much I love my job, and you read between the lines and tell me I'm indispensable, and you couldn't run Bryant & Waites without me."

"You *are* indispensable, and I *couldn't* run Bryant & Waites without you."

Rowan shook his head. "Once more with feeling."

"I don't know what you want me to say, Rowan. I'm feeling as though everything is out of control, and we shouldn't have done what we did, and the one thing which frames my life, my company, is going to be ruined without you there."

Sadness washed over Rowan's expression. "I see."

"What? What do you *see*?" Gideon wished he saw something in what he'd said.

"You don't want me there now. I should have known this would happen." In a smooth, swift move, he removed his seatbelt and slid out of the car, pacing away and leaning on the fence. He had no coat on, and when Gideon followed him, the icy wind was biting.

"I don't understand—"

"You said, and I quote, the company will be ruined without me there, ergo, I'm fired."

"No. I didn't say that. I meant if you leave. If I've fucked things up and you leave."

Rowan turned to face him, his foot up on the bottom rung, his hands forced into his pockets and his skin pale with cold.

"I'm not leaving," Rowan was defiant.

"I'm not asking you to leave," Gideon defended.

They stayed in the face-off for a time, staring at each other until Rowan started to shiver. They bundled back into the car, and Rowan turned it on and cranked the heater, blowing warm air on them. Gideon wanted to lighten the angst going on in here, but he struggled for something light and witty that wouldn't be taken out of context. Rowan came to his rescue, the same as every other time.

"Next time I storm off dramatically remind me to take a coat."

"I will."

Rowan belted up, and Gideon followed suit. Rowan then summed up what was going to happen next. "Let's get home and then maybe we talk, but for now, can we just admit this break was freaking awesome, despite your sore knee, us in bed was fantastic, and neither of us will fuck things up at work."

"Agreed."

Rowan nodded and concentrated on pulling out

onto the road. "I'm turning the music way up so there is no room in the car for thought bubbles."

Gideon couldn't help but snort a laugh at that, and suddenly he felt lighter as if maybe the currently loud Mariah Carey song was drowning out his fears. Halfway home, as he listened to Rowan sing along to Mariah and Wham, and God knows what else appeared to be playing on repeat, he fell asleep. The next thing he knew, just as the dream involving Rowan and the coffee maker in the kitchen was getting to the good bits, Rowan poked at his arm then shook him.

"We're back," he said cheerfully, but not quite meeting Gideon's gaze. Gideon blinked up at his apartment building. "Do you want a hand with your bags? Not that I'm saying you can't lift bags, but your knee—"

Gideon reached over and placed a hand over Rowan's mouth. Sometimes it was the only way to stop the rambling that spilled out.

"Do you want to come in?" Gideon asked softly, and Rowan's eyes widened.

"What are you asking?"

"You know what I'm asking." The dream was still too real, and Rowan was a drug Gideon was slowly becoming addicted to. "Come in, I'll get us a drink, we can talk about what's happening next, and I have some things I think we should cover."

Rowan stared at him for a few seconds, and then he reversed the car to straighten it in the on-street parking and finally he pulled the permit out from the glove box. Gideon had arranged for Rowan to have a permit for when they had meetings after office hours, but he couldn't even recall the last time Rowan had to use it.

That's because you spend as much time as you can at the office to be near Rowan.

Between them they collected his bags from the trunk and hurried up the steps and into the apartment. Gideon fumbled with the key in his icy hands. As soon as the door shut behind them, the warmth of his home surrounded them. He loved this place, solid and stable, and everything he needed when he'd left home. It was also similar to what Luke and him had always dreamed of buying together—a pipe dream but a dream nonetheless. It was weird having Rowan in his place, but there was something happening between them, and Gideon needed time to think things through. He dropped his bag in the hall and hung up his coat, wishing he'd worn it from the car as Rowan did because the temperature had dropped significantly with darkness, and he was ice from the toes up. In the dim light, he realized he could see Rowan staring at him.

"What?" he asked carefully as Rowan took a step closer and went up on tiptoes to cradle his face.

"I don't want to talk," Rowan groaned.

"You want to go home? That's cool, I can—"

Rowan kissed him, forcefully, pressing him back until he was against the wall. "Tell me you have supplies here," he demanded between kisses, and Gideon stopped fighting. They kissed and stumbled toward the bedroom. Rowan knocked his ass against furniture twice before Gideon dragged him close, steadied him in an embrace, and then he forcibly stopped Rowan from moving, bracketing him between Gideon's body and the wall.

"Rowan," he began and then ran out of words.

"In. Me. Now," Rowan said very deliberately and loudly so that Gideon was under no illusion as to what Rowan wanted. The words were the match to the kindling, and somehow they made it into Gideon's bedroom, kissing even as Gideon tried to root around for condoms that he knew he had in his top drawer. He couldn't recall the last time he'd had someone *over*, tending to go to their places or a hotel, but he had to have condoms to go with the ever-present lube. Rowan slapped away his hand and broke the kiss, finding the condoms in the space of a few seconds, and then shoved Gideon onto the bed. Just that single aggressive move had Gideon harder than he'd ever been, and desperate for a taste of Rowan. Typical that his bossy PA was just as bossy in bed when he yanked at Gideon's shoes, pants, socks, shirt, and boxers until Gideon was naked and Rowan was still dressed.

"Jesus," Rowan muttered, staring down at Gideon's cock and rapidly removing his own clothes, dropping condoms and lube to the quilt, and then clambering up to straddle Gideon's thighs. "We need to do this," he added, and Gideon wondered who he was trying to convince. There was desperation in their movements. This wasn't going to be long, slow lovemaking where they took their time. When Rowan slathered lube on his hand and began stretching himself, Gideon had to focus one hundred percent to even get the condom out of the wrapper.

Rowan leaned his head back, arching over Gideon, then collapsed on him and kissed him desperately. The angle meant Gideon's cock slid from Rowan's balls to his hole and back again, over and over, and Gideon could come from this feeling alone.

Rowan shuffled back a little, and then he nodded at Gideon. "In. Me," he growled, and they seemed to come together like magic. As if they were meant to fit. Gideon pressed inside, and Rowan mewled as his body tensed then relaxed. When he was fully seated, Rowan leaned back again, supporting himself with his hands on Gideon's knees, Gideon nearly lost it there and then.

Rowan moved. Slowly at first and then faster as Gideon brought up his knees and Rowan didn't have to support himself. Only then did they meet for awkwardly sloppy kisses that were nothing but lust to drive them higher.

"Fuck," Rowan whined, dropping lower, lifting up, the muscles in his thighs bunching as he moved. "I love this. I love…" Gideon had never seen anything so perfect, so strong, and so sexy. He closed his fingers around Rowan's neglected cock, setting up a counter rhythm so that Rowan fucked down onto Gideon's cock and then up into the fist. He didn't last long, and with a cry, his orgasm blew him apart and streaks of cum painted Gideon's chest and hand. Just that single thing and the ecstasy on Rowan's face was enough to push Gideon over the edge, and he fucked hard into Rowan's tight ass. They stilled as Rowan leaned down and kissed him, and Gideon slowly rocked his hips, chasing the last of the orgasm.

He took care of Rowan, cleaned them up, tucked Rowan into the bed then climbed in himself. He opened his arms and Rowan snuggled in, burying his face in Gideon's neck for the longest time.

"Can we talk now?" Gideon asked. This had the potential to be more serious than just sex, and he needed to make sure they were on the same page.

Rowan yawned. "Unless it's goodnight, can it wait?"

"It can wait."

"Well," he said sleepily. "There we go," he added, and then he seemed to fall asleep, while Gideon held him tight and let sleep take him under too.

What would they talk about in the morning? Gideon wanted to explain about Luke, about his life, about how he was and what he wanted, but what could he possibly say that would make sense of this new connection? They were good in bed. They laughed. They were closer than friends—maybe it was time for Gideon to think long term, and to actually invest his heart in something that wasn't work. He'd lost Luke so many years ago, and he never thought he'd love again, but Rowan was working his way under Gideon's skin, and Gideon didn't want him to leave. Ever.

But when sunlight streamed in past open blinds and woke up Gideon, he reached for Rowan.

Rowan was gone.

FIFTEEN

Rowan

───────────

Rowan held out his hand in front of him, eyeing the key that swung on his middle finger. The morning sunlight caught the metal surface, and he squinted as the light flickered in his eyes. He let the key dangle against his palm, along with the small silver cat keychain it was connected to.

With a sigh, he took out his phone, eyed the text message he'd received that morning from Darcy enquiring how his Christmas had gone.

How had it gone? He'd been able to get closer to Gideon, whether that was a good thing, he still wasn't sure. He had tried his best to stop Gideon from voicing the very concerns he had himself. They'd talked briefly on the ride home, but last night was supposed to have been their opportunity to talk. Really talk. He got the sense that Gideon had something to tell him, but that could be some long-winded reasoning as to why they couldn't be a couple, so instead of talking, Rowan had used his body and distracted Gideon with sex.

Rowan rubbed his brow. He wondered if Gideon had woken up yet. What would he think to find Rowan was gone?

I'm not gone, just…hesitating.

He was crouched on the sidewalk, his back against Gideon's building. The growl of his stomach had driven him outside in search of breakfast. Gideon's refrigerator and cupboards were not so surprisingly empty, considering the Christmas break. He'd always imagined Gideon to be a more eat-out kind of person than a home cook. He had thought it might be some sweet romantic gesture to step out, come back with takeout coffees and rolls filled with tasty breakfast stuff. Having only gotten as far as the street, a blast of fresh air slapped him back to reality. They needed to talk. Rowan wanted Gideon. He also wanted to keep his job. There had always been a hint of flirty fun in their interactions, so he was sure he could walk the line of colleagues and lovers. However, if Gideon decided a relationship wouldn't work, could they really go back to normal, to how they used to be? Could Rowan ignore the things they'd done, the feelings he'd admitted to?

"This makes my head hurt." He bent forward, holding his head in his hands. Or maybe it was his heart that stung the most. He'd admired Gideon, teased him, slowly gotten closer, and now he was there, the chance to be something closer than a PA, and he was freaking out.

I know what I want. I've wanted Gideon for…years. Even when I was with other men, Gideon always had a space in my heart. He lifted his head and stared at the wet sidewalk.

I've always sucked at relationships. Or maybe it was the relationships that sucked. Ones he'd too quickly jumped into because of fickle motives and flimsy emotions from one party or the other. *I should head back inside. Say things properly.*

"Are you okay?" someone said as a shadow cast over him.

Rowan raised his head. Before him stood an elderly woman. She was wrapped warmly in a knee-length coat, scarf, gloves, and fur-lined boots, with bags of shopping in her hands. A taxi pulled away behind her. Rowan smiled, recognizing her as Gideon's neighbor. "Mrs. Hallewell, how are you?"

Her brow furrowed as she looked him over. Rowan had only met her a few times, so he could understand if she didn't know who he was. "Oh, you're Gideon's friend," she said, finally. "The one whose family he was spending Christmas with."

"Yes. Rowan." He used the wall to help him to his feet and slipped Gideon's housekey into his coat pocket. "We got back last night." He bit his lip not entirely sure what the elderly woman knew of Gideon's private affairs. "It was a long drive and it was getting late, so he let me stay over. He's a good boss, always looking out for his staff." He ended with an awkward laugh.

Mrs. Hallewell held out her bags. "Here. Carry these for me." She gave him a stern look. "And Hilda is fine."

Rowan raised an eyebrow at her bluntness but took them without protest.

She sighed heavily as she rummaged inside her handbag for her keys. "My daughter's always telling me how I should get groceries delivered. Honestly, if I didn't go myself, it'd be another reason for me not to leave the house. She'd have me cooped up inside, rotting away."

"I'm sure she's just worried about you." Rowan followed her inside.

She snorted a laugh. "I'm sure, I'm sure. Can you put them in the kitchen for me, please?"

Rowan stopped by the door and went to toe off his shoes.

"You can leave them on, your shoes, just make sure you wipe them well," she called to him from another room.

Scary. Was she psychic? "Sure." He used the doormat then took the bags through to the kitchen, placing them on the end of the counter. A sweet scent hung in the air, her perfume maybe? Mixed with the underlying musty, wooden smell of antique furnishings.

"There you are…"

Rowan couldn't make out everything Hilda was saying, but he could hear her voice. He glanced at the bags. *Should I unpack them for her?*

"Rowan has come to collect you." Hilda walked into the kitchen and in her arms, she held Gideon's cat, Kimi. "I'm sure Gideon's missed you." She pressed her face into Kimi's white and gray fur. "Here you go." She closed the gap, passing Kimi to Rowan.

"Erm." Rowan took the cat in his arms. "Okay." He hadn't interacted with Kimi much, the blue-eyed Ragdoll favoring Gideon's attention over a guest's. Rowan was grateful Kimi didn't struggle and settled against him. He hugged her to him. She was warm, and her purrs vibrated through his chest above his heart. "Are you sure it's okay for me to take her?"

"Why wouldn't it be? You work for him, right?"

"I thought you might—"

She waved her hand. "He'll be around soon enough to thank me. He'll have been missing her." She scratched beneath Kimi's chin, the cat lifting her head, purring more loudly. "He might have trouble outwardly showing his affections for others, but I can tell how much he loves her." She looked at Rowan. "The way he smiles when he's with her. I've only seen him smiling that way around one other person." She looked pointedly at Rowan then patted Kimi's head. "If you'll excuse me, I need to call my daughter and tell her I'm home. She'll worry herself silly one of these days." Hilda shook her head, pointing to the shopping bags as she walked away. "Thank you for your help. You can see yourself out."

Rowan looked down at Kimi, who returned his gaze. Her blue eyes conveyed her impatience as if questioning why Rowan was still standing around and telling him to leave already. "Fine," he said, gently stroking the length of her back. "Let's get you home."

Rowan headed back to Gideon's, fumbling with the door as he tried to juggle the cat and fish the keys from his pocket. Once inside, he lingered in the entrance, listening. Was Gideon awake? Kimi squirmed for her freedom, and Rowan leaned down, allowing her to jump from his arms. He watched as she made a beeline for the kitchen. He followed slowly behind her, peeking around the corner to find Gideon sitting at the breakfast bar, staring at a mug in his hands and the contents he appeared to be nursing. A frown creased his brow.

Gideon looked down when Kimi nudged his ankle. "Kimi? What are you…" He trailed off when he spotted Rowan.

"Hey," Rowan said and raised his hand. "Morning."

"I thought…" Gideon leaned down and picked up Kimi. "I thought you'd left."

"I went to get breakfast."

"Was it tasty?" He tilted his head.

Rowan glanced at his empty hands. "Ah. I didn't get very far."

Gideon smoothed his hand over Kimi's head and smiled. "Hilda grabbed you." His shoulders relaxed as if coming to terms with the fact Rowan hadn't run away.

Rowan decided it was easier to agree. He stepped into the kitchen and came to stand beside the counter. "So, last night was…"

He braced himself but Gideon didn't say anything.

At least he didn't say it was a mistake.

"Do you want to talk about it? Us? What we do going forward?" Everything inside him was screaming for him to stop, but they needed to figure out their relationship. Whatever that might be.

"I do, but…" He hugged Kimi.

"But?" Rowan clasped his hands together.

"Can we do it once I finish my coffee?" Gideon grinned.

Rowan dropped his head forward and closed his eyes. "Coffee sounds like a great idea." He slid onto the second stool and leaned his elbows on the edge of the counter while Gideon poured him a mug. They sat quietly together, Gideon fussing over Kimi, who had settled on his lap and Rowan watched them.

His smile really is brighter when Kimi is around. He wondered how he hadn't noticed that before. *Too busy focusing on work.* Until now the only reason for him to enter Gideon's home.

"So, where do we start?" Gideon pushed his empty mug away from him.

Rowan ran his fingertips up and down the side of his as he considered what to say. "First, can we just make sure we're on the same page? Forget about whatever anxieties you have about the company and work stuff. Do you want to have a relationship with me? A relationship that isn't that of a boss and his PA?"

Sex with Gideon had been great, but if that was all that was on the table, he couldn't go along with it. Not this time. Not Gideon.

Gideon stroked Kimi's back. "It's been a long time since I entered into a relationship with someone. Something serious. Because of various reasons that wasn't what I wanted." He looked at Rowan.

"Do you want to tell me about it?"

Gideon nodded then stared down at Kimi, who purred like a train.

"I had this boyfriend." He looked up at Rowan, his blue eyes bright with emotion. "Actually, I need to be completely honest with you, otherwise what's the point? I met him in college, and he was more than just a friend. He was my *best* friend, my lover. His name was Luke Waites."

Rowan's eyes widened. "Waites? As in Bryant & Waites? You told me that you made that part up to make the company sound good."

"I lied. It was a joint idea to build a company. Luke and I were both fresh out of college with our shiny degrees in business, and hopelessly in love. We wanted to do something different than to end up in an office."

"How did you get the idea for hiring out boyfriends?"

Gideon half-smiled. "Luke's friend needed to produce a boyfriend out of thin air to go to a party, and Luke volunteered me. I could have killed him, but it went okay, and the germ of an idea of setting up a company that hired out boyfriends on a professional basis was born. Of course, there was a lot of tequila involved in the conception of the company. It had been Luke's idea to begin with—thus the Waites part of the name. Only Luke never saw our ideas become reality."

"What happened?" Rowan laced their fingers and held tight after grief washed over Gideon's expression— something Rowan had never seen in him before.

"The night before my birthday, he proposed and I said yes, and we had the most amazing Christmas, you know the kind of special day that stays with you forever?" He waited for Rowan's reaction and Rowan nodded. "The evening after Christmas Day everything changed. He had this bike, an old Harley he'd been fixing up. It was snowing, and they're not sure what happened, but the accident was fast and brutal. He never saw the car…"

Rowan gasped. "Oh God, I'm so sorry." Rowan was

choked up at the grief he could feel in Gideon now. What a tragic waste, what a loss to a young man on his first steps out into the world.

"I felt as if my heart had been severed, and I was broken. It took me a long time to get on track and to build Bryant & Waites into something real as a way of honoring Luke. The pain of his loss has lessened to become an ache in my chest, but it can still hurt even after all this time. Particularly on Christmas. It was twenty years ago now, but I will never forget him."

"Why would you? He's as much a part of you as your blue eyes."

Gideon slid his hand from Rowan's, leaned over, and kissed him gently as if he'd needed Rowan to be that understanding.

"I never thought I'd let what I had with Luke stop me from living, not until you walked into my office for your interview seven years ago, and now it's all I can think about. Without realizing it, I shut down that side of myself because losing Luke was like losing a limb, and I didn't want to go through that again."

"Okay." Rowan gripped his empty mug.

"I guess getting to spend time with you, and your family, made me realize having people in my life might not be such a bad thing."

Rowan eased his grip. "So you're saying…"

"Yes. I'm saying, yes, I want to be in a relationship with you." He smiled. "And that scares me a little."

"I swear boyfriend-me and PA-me are two very different people," Rowan said with an embarrassed chuckle.

Gideon nodded. "I think I get that having spent time with you these last few days. But dating PA-you isn't what scares me, not in that way at least." He sighed. "If watching my parents has taught me anything it's that when relationships end, people can become petty, and if —and I mean *if* because nobody knows what'll happen in the future—the relationship ends, I don't want to be like them. I don't want to end up petty."

"You're not like your parents," Rowan said then bit his lip. He knew nothing about them.

Gideon tilted his head. "If I'm being honest, I don't think I am either. But relationships and love and…it can make people crazy, right? You've said plenty of times how much you love your job, and even though I'd like to think we could carry on the same, even if things ended, I just don't know. Maybe being an asshole is embedded in my DNA."

Rowan pursed his lips and considered what Gideon had said on top of his revelations about Luke. "I've been your PA for a while now. After a string of failed attempts at carving a career for myself, this job was a breath of fresh air. I finally found something I was interested in. A big part of loving my job is because of you. Of course, there's other stuff, the clients, the boyfriends, the various companies we work with, and filing. God, how I love filing," he added in a sarcastic tone.

"Ah, yes, I think you might have mentioned that or rather the exact opposite a few times over the years."

"If you're scared, then I'll be brave for both of us. I'm willing to risk you becoming an asshole, assuming this…" he waved his hand between the two of them "…

goes downhill faster than you being knocked off your feet by Bear. I love my job. I want to keep it, but if I were to choose, if I have to choose right now…then I want to take a chance on us being together. We can take it slow, as slow as you need, that way we can keep your petty gene from activating, and if we need to, we can back out, end things with minimal damage to our working relationship, and—"

"Rowan," Gideon interrupted.

"What?"

He crooked his finger, beckoning Rowan toward him, to move closer. "Shut up," he said with a smirk when Rowan was within his reach. He tugged the front of Rowan's shirt, encouraging him forward until they were close enough to kiss.

The kiss was gentle, slow, and Rowan let out a soft sigh as he was silenced.

Gideon nibbled Rowan's lower lip then pulled away and held Rowan's gaze. "I already said yes, didn't I?"

Rowan looked up at the ceiling. "That was a yes? A genuine one? But you said—" Gideon grabbed him, kissing him harder.

"I said it was scary, but I'm going to do it anyway."

Rowan wrapped his hand around Gideon's. "You mean we're going to do it?"

"Yeah." Gideon pressed a kiss to Rowan's cheek. "We are."

Rowan rested his forehead to Gideon's. "Together."

SIXTEEN

Gideon

Gideon had no clue what to do next, even with Rowan in his arms and the bedroom only a few feet away. His entire relationship with Luke had been based around college, youthful exploration, and a bright shining hope for a grand future. Relationships since then had been short lived, based mostly around sex, and with not much in the way of dating as such. He could easily slip into that with Rowan, but he wanted this to be different, not only because he was putting everything on the line but because what they had must mean something more.

"We should go out for brunch," he announced just as Kimi leaped up onto his shoulders and began kneading his hair.

"That sounds so grown up," Rowan teased and extricated himself from Gideon's hold carefully so that Kimi didn't lose her grip. If Gideon thought it was even possible, he fell a little harder then. *Love me, love my cat.*

"I know this place, it's nothing fancy but the bacon is always crisp and the pancakes—"

Rowan kissed him to stop him from talking. "You had me at bacon. Can I get a shower first?" He glanced sideways at the suitcase which sat inside the door and raised an eyebrow in question.

"Yeah, sure, sorry…go for it…I'll go after——"

Another kiss to keep him quiet. If this was going to be how Rowan got Gideon to finish sentences, then it was going to get awkward in the office.

"How about we save water?" Rowan asked, but he was already backing up to the bathroom, tugging Gideon with him so fast that Kimi meowed loudly then grumbled and sulked as she leaped down and curled up on the sofa. Water plus Rowan? It was a no-brainer.

One bathroom blowjob later, with both of them smelling of Gideon's shower gel, they finally got dressed, and Rowan was looking a long way past smug.

"It was one bet," Gideon grumped, wishing he'd never suggested who could hold out the longest. But *come on*…seeing Rowan on his knees and looking up at him and doing that *thing* with his tongue, and then his wandering fingers…no one would be able to keep their orgasm at bay, let alone Gideon, who had fantasies about Rowan on his knees.

Sue me, it's Rowan, and he's hot.

Stepping outside of the apartment and then onto the street into the cold biting wind was a shock to the system. Inside they'd just been the two of them where reality didn't intrude, but out here it was obvious everything had changed, not least of which was Rowan reaching for Gideon's gloved hand.

"We don't have to…I mean it's only down here,"

Gideon said and had to sidestep around a woman walking a dog, narrowly avoiding having to make a scene about not taking Rowan's hand. Only he wasn't getting away from it as Rowan moved swiftly in front of him and blocked his way before kissing him soundly in front of whoever the hell was looking from whatever window.

Well. That was that then.

This time he took Rowan's hand, despite how awkward it was with the bulky gloves and the fact that they only had to walk two blocks to The Bean. They'd have to talk about boundaries in the office later but holding hands as they ate pancakes and bacon one-handed whilst grinning at each other like idiots was clearly the new normal.

Rowan slid around to snuggle in next to Gideon. *Is this what it was like to have a boyfriend now? To hug and kiss and snuggle in public? I've been missing out on so much.* Gideon even ignored the looks and simply smiled at everyone who glanced at them. Not that people knew he was cuddling with another man who was his PA. To them this was just boyfriends on a coffee date, and that wasn't something that caused much of an issue. Not one of them knew the weight of what they were doing.

"So that's date one." Rowan patted his belly and gave a full body sigh.

"I thought date one was staying in the same cabin."

"No, that was a pre-date as in it pre-dated us deciding to give things a go." He chuckled before sipping fresh coffee.

"It's your turn to organize date two," Gideon was

decisive.

The check arrived, and they tussled for a moment before Rowan distracted Gideon with another kiss and stole it from the table. "I win again."

"That's cheating."

"Get used to it, Gids."

"You called me Gids." Gideon shrugged on his heavy coat and wondered exactly how he felt about that. Plenty of people in his life had attempted to shorten his name but Gideon had never liked it. Until Rowan.

"Is that an issue?" Rowan asked seriously as he wrapped a scarlet scarf around his neck.

Gideon considered the question and then shook his head. "I like it."

"Okay then, Gids, my sexy lover." He waggled his eyebrows suggestively. "Follow me."

It wasn't so much following him as being tugged out of the shop and then dragged down the street and up East 9th street. They ended up in Greenwich Village at the arch into Washington Square Park. It was a big space, formed from a lot of pathways with grass between them, but it wasn't its usual busy self. Most of that had to be due to the fact that icy wind blew around the buildings, collecting snow and blasting it in people's faces. They couldn't talk much into the wind, but finally they found a bench under a leafless sugar maple, and the wind was partially blocked by the tree.

"This is a good date," Gideon murmured, wondering where that came from as he was sitting in a cold park, on a freezing bench, in a bitter wind, wrapped up so only his eyes were visible.

Rowan snuggled in again as he'd done at the coffee shop, and Gideon knew with certainty that it was being with Rowan that made it a good date. His cell vibrated in his pocket, but there was no way he was taking off his gloves, let alone rooting through his coat until they were back in the office or at home. His job was twenty-four-seven and who knew when someone would have issues on a booking, but he was having this morning off.

They sat in silence for a while, and then Rowan began chatting about family and dogs, and every so often Gideon would ask questions. Only halfway through a story involving Deon and Dog and an unfortunate roast chicken that had met a canine end, he went quiet.

"Are you okay?" Gideon imagined he'd messed up by not getting more involved in the conversation, but there was something about Rowan's voice, and he was mesmerized. *I should have said more, kept up my end of the conversation.*

"So I have an admission," Rowan began.

Gideon's chest tightened. This didn't sound good. In the scale of one to complete shit, this sounded like an admission that he was already dating or married or—

"I'm going to have to rename Deon," he said and inched away from Gideon to meet his gaze head on.

"Why?" Gideon wasn't sure why he asked because Rowan was so damn serious.

"You want to know why I called her Deon?"

"Because you have a thing for Canadian divas who sing the theme tunes to sinking boat movies?" Gideon went for a joke, but Rowan pulled his scarf away from his lips and shook his head.

"When he ended up at the house, it was Dog who was the life and soul of the party. I mean, it was Dog who got the chicken from the counter. It's Dog who led the great Easter charge against the chocolate eggs and ended up needing a veterinarian. Deon was always quiet, kind of grumpy, serious, untouchable, as if he didn't want to be part of our world."

"Sounds…interesting."

"Don't hate me," Rowan began and held up gloved hands.

"That's not the sentence I was expecting to hear on only our second date," Gideon joked.

"I named him after you, Gideon. Deon mostly because he was grumpy."

"Oh." Gideon wanted to feel hurt, but how could he when Rowan was looking so miserable.

"You have to know because the family knows, and they'll tell you one day, and you'll be pissed at me, and you know what?" He leaned toward Gideon.

"What?" How could this story get any better? Or worse?

"You're not grumpy, you've never really been because a few days after I started working for you, I had a handle on you, and you're just cautious." He sat back in triumph.

"Not grumpy, just cautious," Gideon repeated the facts as he saw them and stared right at Rowan. He held his gaze, wanting desperately to tease a smile, but he couldn't stop the snort of laughter.

"No wonder Deon loves me. He has my awesome name."

"You're not pissed?"

"Why would I be pissed?" He held out an arm and Rowan slid close and into a hug. "I love you. You're an idiot, and Deon adores me."

Rowan said something into Gideon's coat that didn't make sense and then eased himself away. "You love me?"

Well shit. He hadn't meant it to slip out quite like that. Not in a frozen park with them both wrapped up in so many layers they were buried worse than hibernating animals. He'd imagined saying the words over dinner or maybe in bed or—

Rowan pounced on him as much as he could in his huge coat and yanked at Gideon's scarf until he could find his lips to kiss him soundly. Then he sat back with a satisfied grin on his face.

"Well, hell," he began with a broad smile that reached his brown eyes. "Gids, I love you too."

———

Gideon found waking up next to Rowan was an interesting experience. He had this way of sprawling out and taking up the entire bed, and Gideon couldn't love it more. They'd said the words over and over when they made love, when they had snacks at midnight, and just before they fell asleep in each other's arms, with Kimi curled up on the pillow by their heads.

The fact that Kimi bopped Rowan's nose before he

snuggled down just added extra points in the Rowan-is-great list.

But waking up today, there was a weight on Gideon's chest, and he couldn't shake it at all, knowing why it was there but not sure how to fix things.

"Can I show you something?" he asked post shower sex and when they were both dressed and sipping hot coffee.

"Didn't you already do that?" Rowan deadpanned, and Gideon shook his head.

"Something other than my dick."

Rowan pouted. "That's disappointing."

"It's not going to be easy to show you, but I need to, for me, and for you."

"Okay, sure." Rowan didn't look worried, but he hugged Gideon as if he sensed that Gideon needed it.

The drive to the cemetery wasn't a long one, with light traffic it was under two hours to get out of New York City and head up the coast to Milford. To his credit, Rowan didn't once ask where they were going, instead he kept up a steady list of stories about his family and alternated those with finding music that wasn't an insult to his ears. At least that's what he called Gideon's container of CDs before syncing his phone and using Spotify. He had eclectic tastes in music from Aretha Franklin to AC/DC, but that was Rowan.

When they reached the cemetery gates and pulled off the road, Rowan turned off all the music and was instantly respectful. They exchanged glances with Rowan nodding his head once. Gideon didn't have to recall where to walk to find Luke, he came here every year after Christmas, and sometimes in between if he wanted to center his life for some reason. Rowan didn't immediately reach for Gideon's hand, but Gideon sought his hold, and with gloves off, they laced their fingers and headed across the icy grass.

"Twenty years," Gideon whispered as they passed markers for people who'd died recently. "The passage of time is marked by the number of graves I pass to get to him." Rowan was quiet, but that was okay because it was Gideon's turn to talk. They reached the gravestone. "Luke Waites, taken too soon, cherished son, brother, and friend." Reading the words, as he always did, he waited for the crushing weight of grief and loneliness, but for some reason, this time it wasn't there.

"Hi, Luke, I'm Rowan." Rowan didn't say anything else, just simply stood quietly, gripping Gideon's hand.

"Luke, I met someone. This is Rowan, I've told you about him before. I finally pulled the stick out of my ass and told him how I felt. I love him."

"And I love him too," Rowan added after a short pause.

Gideon pressed a kiss to the tip of Rowan's nose. Rowan tipped his chin, and they shared the briefest, most gentle kiss.

And in the frozen graveyard, the whisper of snow swirling around them felt like a message, as if Luke was okay with Gideon and Rowan.

And Gideon knew that the rest of his life was just beginning, with Rowan at his side.

Epilogue

The sound of fireworks echoed from outside. Gideon turned his head, checked on Kimi, who was curled up on a footstool, unperturbed by the New Year celebrations.

"Curled up same as Rowan." He gently stroked back Rowan's hair, smiled at the small trembles of Rowan's lips as he breathed against Gideon's chest. "I thought we were supposed to see the New Year in together." He pressed his cheek to the top of Rowan's head. Part of him wanted to tease him, mess with him and stir him awake, and yet, he didn't.

It had been a year and a few days since they had entered into a relationship no longer merely that of a boss and his PA, and Gideon's only regret was that they hadn't done so sooner. He closed his eyes, hugged Rowan to him, appreciating the closeness of a warm body, but not just anyone's…Rowan's. This had become one of his favorite things, even more so in the last four months.

Being able to go to bed and then wake each morning with Rowan beside him still amazed Gideon.

We're together. Every. Single. Day.

After months of Gideon asking, Rowan had finally agreed to move in with him.

You see me every day at the office. You really want to live together as well? Rowan had said each time and had given Gideon a look, a look that said Rowan knew Gideon had, up to that point, enjoyed his own space and questioned whether he was really ready for someone to insert themselves into his home. Their belongings mixing with his and bringing with them routines and habits that might clash with his own.

"I'm glad I didn't give up." He leaned forward and kissed Rowan's forehead. *Wake up. I've something important to ask you.*

They had spent Christmas with Rowan's family again this year. Gideon thought he'd seen everything there was about the chaotic family but apparently, he was wrong. This time he was officially considered to be part of the family which meant more mom-hugs, more dog fussing, awkward sibling conversations, and children deciding *Uncle* Gideon was now fair game to include in their play.

Thank God I learned my lesson from last year and left the suits at home.

Over the few days visit, he'd been faced with muddy paws, chocolate-covered small hands, and spilled paint, and he'd loved every minute. He smiled to himself and stared at the muted television at a band he didn't recognize singing in the New Year.

A year, huh? Should I take Rowan to visit my parents?

Last January he'd contacted his parents alone. A brisk phone call to his dad and a short visit to his mom's, wishing them good health for another year. His mom, as he'd expected, talked non-stop about the new baby. The new grandchild in her "new" family, although it wasn't exactly new as she'd been with her current husband, Mark, for eleven years. It just wasn't family Gideon was part of, nor was invited to be part of. He wondered how she would react if he brought Rowan with him. Would she put on her fake loving mother warmth ?

Do I care? Seemed Rowan came with as much family as a person could handle. Beautiful and warm, full of laughter and smiles.

Rowan alone would be enough for Gideon to call family, and he wanted to show him that. Gideon pressed his hand to his pants' pocket to the spot where he was carrying a ring.

How long have I been holding onto this?

He'd been looking for an opportunity to propose to Rowan for days, weeks. At first, he was going to do it before they went away for Christmas, just the two of them. Then he decided he wanted to do the whole asking the parents' permission thing and to do so in person. Gill had cried. Jodie had slapped him on the back, and all three of them were nearly caught when Deon lured Rowan into the kitchen having whined for treats.

The more Gideon thought about proposing, the more nervous he had gotten. He'd kind of chickened out of doing it while surrounded by Rowan's family. And even now he was embarrassed at the thought of going down on one knee in front of a crowd. It had taken him months to get Rowan to agree to live with him, would getting him to say yes to marriage be the same?

I'll ask him every day if I have to. He clutched the ring. Assuming he had the courage to ask a first time.

Rowan's cell phone hummed on the arm of the couch, and Gideon was surprised when Rowan gave a heavy sigh.

"You were awake?"

"No." He sat up and reached for his phone. "Well, maybe a thought bubble or two ago. You think too loud."

"You're still doing that?"

Only to me.

The bubbles seemed to be a habit Rowan had developed to tease him and him alone.

Something just between us, even back then.

"Yep." Rowan flashed his teeth as he grinned and looked at his cell.

Gideon sighed. Bubbles weren't the only thing between them now. There was so much about them, between them only the other got to see.

Rowan quirked his eyebrow. "Oh, it's Jared." He raised a hand to stop Gideon from speaking as he answered the call.

"Hello? Yep, I can talk."

"Jared? Everything okay?" Gideon said in a low voice. If he remembered correctly, Jared was meant to be with a client that evening.

"Happy New Year to you too. So, what's up?"

Rowan slid away from Gideon and got to his feet. "You're where?" He lowered the phone and told Gideon, "I'm going to take this in the bedroom."

Gideon nodded, turning his head when Kimi jumped up onto the arm of the couch. "And you're awake too, huh?" He picked her up and put her on his lap, stroking the length of her back. "What do you think? Should I ask him tonight?"

Kimi purred loudly, pawing his lap before settling across his thighs.

"That a yes?" He chuckled.

"Yes, what?" Rowan suddenly appeared.

"That was quick."

Rowan dropped back down on the couch with a huff. "I love Jared but seriously sometimes I wish he'd stop being so nice."

"There a problem?"

Through his time with them, Jared had become a popular boyfriend at the company, particularly in the last two years. He was good natured, diligent, charming, a little too laid-back at times, but that made him easy to work with and able to fit into whatever situation the client desired.

Rowan winced. "Not really a problem. However, I do need to call him back in fifteen minutes."

"Okay. Why?"

"Exit plan. Pretend family emergency."

"And why do you need to do this?"

"I'm not a hundred percent sure, but I think he said he ended up agreeing to an offer of a foursome."

"Four? How?"

"He wasn't on the call long enough to explain."

Gideon blinked and stared at the moving picture on the television as he tried to imagine how someone even found themselves in the position to be offered something like that. "Foursome," he uttered.

"Have you ever done anything like that? A threesome or anything?" Rowan flipped his cell over in his hands.

"No. The opportunity never really came up."

Rowan chuckled. "Same." He pointed to himself. "Besides, I'm more than enough for any man to handle all by my lonesome." He sat back and Gideon leaned over, pressing a kiss to his cheek.

"You are." Gideon blew a breath. "Which reminds me, there's something I want to ask you."

"Ask me?"

"Yes." It felt as if it were a now or never kind of moment for his proposal. He had to stop putting it off. Rowan was the man for him. The one he wanted his forever with.

Rowan smiled and gently lifted Kimi from Gideon's lap. She meowed when he placed her on the floor, then padded off toward the kitchen. "I kind of have something I want to ask you too. Ever since Christmas."

Gideon swallowed. "Really?"

"Mmm." Rowan shuffled closer and took hold of Gideon's hand. "But you should go first."

Something to ask me? Rowan looked serious. "No, it's fine. Ask what you want to ask." Gideon rested his other hand over Rowan's.

"Okay." Rowan pouted his lips. "Then, how about

we go at the same time?" He bounced a little on the cushion as he closed the gap and straightened his back.

"Together?"

"Yeah." Rowan smiled brightly. "I'll count to three and then after three, we both say what we were going to."

Gideon nodded. This was fine.

"Okay, so…" Rowan looked him in the eye. "One. Two. Three."

Gideon closed his eyes and blurted out, "Let's get married."

"Let's get a dog," Rowan said at the same time.

Gideon opened his eyes. "Dog?"

Rowan didn't say anything. His eyes were wide as he stared through Gideon.

"Rowan?"

Color flushed Rowan's cheeks.

"Hey. You all right?" Gideon waved his hand in front of Rowan's face.

"You…you want to…" Rowan bit his lip. "Marry. You said marry, right?"

Gideon sucked on his teeth. "Erm, no. I said… let's…" *I can't think of anything.* "So, a dog? You want a dog?"

"Yes. If I could I'd bring Deon home, but it wouldn't be fair to split the pack now. Plus, Momo was on about someone they knew just had puppies that they'd need homes for, and I thought—" He hit Gideon on the chest. "Forget the dog. You totally said you wanted to get married."

"I did?"

"You did!" Rowan got to his knees, straddled Gideon's thighs, and pinched his nipple beneath his shirt.

"All right. Okay. I did. I did." He grabbed Rowan's hand, with his other he reached into his pocket and pulled out the ring. "I've wanted to ask you for a while. Never felt the moment was quite right. I wanted it to be perfect, but in the end, it turned out like this—"

Rowan covered Gideon's mouth. "It is perfect. You said it once about my family. Perfectly chaotic, right? So, to me, this is…" He smiled, cupped Gideon's jaw with his free hand, then leaned in and kissed him. "The absolute best proposal I could have ever gotten." He kissed him some more, a slow, firm kiss that Gideon wanted to melt into and stay that way, connected for eternity.

"I love you," Gideon said, raising Rowan's hand and slipping the ring on his finger, relieved that it pushed down over Rowan's knuckle. *It fit.* "Marry me?" he said and rested his hands on Rowan's waist.

Rowan held up his hand, staring at the ring. Light bounced off the platinum band, a small leaf pattern etched around it. "You're sure?" he asked. "Like, properly sure?"

Gideon gripped Rowan tightly, raised his hips so his crotch pushed back against Rowan's ass. "I am. Never been surer."

Rowan grinned. "So I see." He lowered his hand between them and rubbed Gideon's hard dick through his clothes as he squirmed on top of him.

I want him. All of him. Always.

"Okay," Rowan said as he stilled. He pulled back his hand, declaring, "I need to tell my moms."

"Seriously." Gideon leaned back as Rowan jumped up. "And wait, shouldn't you be saying something to me first?"

"Like what?"

"Well, I don't want to be presumptuous, but a *yes* would be nice."

"What? I didn't say it?"

Gideon shook his head.

With a smile, Rowan leaned down and held Gideon's face as he kissed him. The kiss was deep as he slid his tongue over Gideon's. He breathed in deeply and pulled back, opened his mouth, hesitated but then smirked, saying, "I'll tell you later. In bed." He tilted his head and picked up his phone. "Right now, I need to text everybody."

"I hate you," Gideon expressed, lifting his hips as he rearranged the front of his pants.

"Not what your bubble is saying." Rowan pointed to the empty space above Gideon's head. "It's all hearts and blushing emojis." He scrolled through his cell.

Gideon couldn't argue with that observation; his heart and head were full of Rowan. "Oh," he quipped as he realized something.

"Hmm? What?" Rowan looked up from his phone.

"Jared."

Rowan froze then comically slapped his forehead. "Oh my God. What time is it? Gah." He rushed from the room as he made the call.

"I'm so sorry," Gideon heard him say when Jared answered.

Leaning his head back, Gideon stared at the pattern of light on the ceiling. He could hear Rowan in the other room. In the office, Rowan was organized, on top of everything. At home, he was kind of an airhead, preferring to take things as they came. He smiled when Rowan erupted into laughter.

Gideon picked up the remote and turned off the television. He got to his feet, switched off lights as he made his way to the bedroom eager to hear Rowan's answer, though he was ninety-nine percent sure he knew what it was. There was always that one percent of unpredictability when it came to Rowan. He nudged open the door, his chest tightening as he laid eyes on Rowan's shining eyes, his nose crinkling as he laughed.

"I have to go," Rowan said. "I'll let you tell Gideon yourself when you're in the office next. Yes. Goodnight. Be safe and Happy New Year." He hung up. "Sorry about that."

Gideon shook his head. "Problem solved?"

"Yes." Rowan placed his cell on the nightstand.

Never change.

Gideon walked up to Rowan and wrapped him in a hug. "I love you," he said.

"Me too." Rowan hugged him back then mumbled into the crook of his neck, "Yes, in case it wasn't already obvious. My answer is yes." He gripped Gideon's back with warm hands. Gideon closed his eyes and it was as if a light glowed inside him, bright, happy, warm. Together with Rowan, they could be a family.

My precious PA.

He pressed a kiss to Rowan's forehead.

And one day…my husband.

Get the next book here - Jared

Jared (Boyfriend for Hire 4)

Jared

Jared's world is turned upside down after Luka hands over his pocket money to hire him as a friend for his lonely, widowed dad.

Jared is good at his job, but his soft heart means that he often finds himself in the weirdest of situations. A kind-of-threesome, a disappearing swan, and a destroyed hotel room are just the tip of the iceberg, but he is a popular boyfriend-for-hire and always in demand. He dreams of working as a family psychologist one day, and as his work with Bryant & Waites is funding his studies, the last thing he wants is to lose his job. At a make-or-break meeting, Jared vows to focus on being strictly professional. Still, almost immediately, he meets Luka sitting on the office steps with pocket money in hand and with a sadness that melts Jared's resolve. Luka explains that his mom passed away some years ago, and his hardworking father needs a friend. Jared has no intention of taking Luka's pocket money, but he wants to make Luka smile again, and if being hired as a friend for Luka's widowed dad is what it takes, then he's all in.

Being a single dad to eleven-year-old Luka is the best thing in Nate's world, but add running a bar with long hours, and his work-life balance is screwed. There's certainly no time for relationships, and even though Luka worries about his dad's love life daily, romance is the last thing on Nate's agenda. Owning Rhea's Bar and keeping his head above water is second only to his love for Luka. His entire world consists of his son and the bar until Jared stumbles into his life. Even though Nate won't admit it, he's lonely, and Jared is the first friend he's made in a very long time. Could their friendship become something more?

Sapphire Cay

Sapphire Cay

1. Follow the Sun
2. Under the Sun
3. Chase The Sun
4. Christmas In The Sun
5. Capture The Sun
6. Forever In The Sun

Also from RJ & Meredith

Standalone Christmas

- The Road to Frosty Hollow

Free Reads

- Stronger Together

Meet RJ Scott

RJ discovered romance in books at a very young age and realized that if there wasn't romance on the page, she could create it in her head. With over one hundred and fifty books published, she is a full time author of gay romance.

She lives and works out of her home in the beautiful English countryside, spends her spare time reading, watching films, and enjoying time with her family.

The last time she had a week's break from writing she didn't like it one little bit and has yet to meet a box of chocolates she couldn't defeat.

www.rjscott.co.uk | rj@rjscott.co.uk

NEWSLETTER - rjscott.co.uk/rjnews

facebook.com/author.rjscott

instagram.com/rjscott_author

amazon.com/author/rj-scott

bookbub.com/authors/rj-scott

goodreads.com/rjscott

patreon.com/RJScott

Meet Meredith Russell

Meredith Russell lives in the heart of England. An avid fan of many story genres, she enjoys nothing less than a happy ending. She believes in heroes and romance and strives to reflect this in her writing. Sharing her imagination and passion for stories and characters is a dream Meredith is excited to turn into reality.

www.meredithrussell.co.uk
meredithrussell666@gmail.com

facebook.com/meredithrussellauthor
x.com/MeredithRAuthor
instagram.com/miss_meredith_r